Arty and the Texas Ranger

Arty and the Texas Ranger

By
Mark L. Redmond

Illustrated by
Laura Ury

SWORD of the LORD PUBLISHERS

P. O. Box 1099, Murfreesboro, TN 37133

Printed and Bound in the United States of America

CHAPTER ONE

Bill Munson, our foreman, had brought some letters with him when he returned from doing some errands in town. Half an hour later when I walked into our parlor, Ma was sitting at her writing desk with a letter in front of her, and she was crying. Wondering who had died, I rushed across the room and knelt beside her. Putting my arms around her, I tried to ease her grief.

She smiled through her tears and handed me the letter. Quickly I read, looking for bad news and checking the signature. The letter was from Grandma and Grandpa Delaney in Kentucky telling us that they were coming to visit us. Ma had been crying because she was happy.

I threw the letter into the air, jumped up and let out a whoop, then squeezed Ma until she could barely breathe. Then I picked up the scattered pages, and we began to calculate. The letter was three weeks old. Allowing for breakdowns and weather problems, Ma figured they should arrive in about four days.

I knew I couldn't stand the wait. I looked at Ma, who was still crying, and wondered if I'd ever understand women.

We hadn't seen my grandparents in over four years. Ma was very close to them, and I knew she was as excited as I was at the news of their coming. We had visited them in Kentucky when I was eight, and Grandpa had made that visit one I'd never forget. We had spent hours together hunting, fishing and watching forest creatures that almost never seemed to be afraid of us.

Pa had been there with us; how I wished he could be with us again. Three years had passed, but I still clearly remembered the fire that had destroyed our general store and killed Pa. My heart ached sometimes, especially at night when I awoke from a dream that Pa was still alive and we were together again.

I didn't cry easily, but I always cried after one of those dreams.

I was now fourteen years old. During the two years Ma and I had been in Texas, I had learned to ride and track like an Indian, defend myself with my fists and feet, handle a gun or a knife as well as some men and survive in some of the toughest parts of Texas. I was Miss Ross's best student in reading and writing, and only one or two of my friends could beat me in spelling or ciphering.

Now I know that all my talk about being able to ride and track and fight and shoot probably sounds like nothing but wind passing through leaky organ bellows, but it's the truth. I'm not bragging either. I give most of the credit to those who taught me those things and to the Lord who let me learn them so easily. Why, even the book-learning part came easy to me. Esther Travis, who was in school with me and a really good friend—for a girl—said it wasn't fair for a person to pick up so much so fast with so little effort. It wasn't that I didn't have to try; I just didn't have to try very hard to get most things.

Chad, our top hand, had been teaching me to shoot and fight. Although I'd grown four inches and gained fifteen pounds while Chad was training and working with me, he could outfight, out-shoot, outride and outwork me before breakfast and not even break out in a sweat.

When Chad had agreed—with Ma's permission—to start teaching me how to fight, I had been excited. But that excitement had left me in a hurry when I found that my "training," as Chad called it, would include splitting and stacking firewood and running at a slow pace for hours. He always grinned and said he was going to make an Indian out of me.

Meanwhile, Marshal Luke Bodie, who rode out to the ranch at least twice a week with some excuse but who really came to see Ma, kept giving me pointers to help me shoot better. He had given me my first pistol, a new one that shot bullets with metal casings instead of an old Colt like the one that our cook Grubby carried. His was a cap-and-ball pistol that seemed as if it would have to be slow and awkward, but in Grubby's hands it wasn't either one.

While the men were training me in what Bill always called "cowboy savvy," Ma and Miss Ross, who had become best friends, were working on my book learning. In addition to the regular school-work that I did, they made sure I was always reading a book.

Now, that may sound like a complaint, but it isn't. I liked nothing better than to saddle Prince early on a summer morning and ride off with something to eat, a fishing pole or some extra cartridges, or both, and a good book. I always let Ma know where I'd be so she wouldn't worry. About the time the sun came up, I'd be at either my favorite fishing hole or in the canyon where I practiced shooting.

The first thing I always did at either place was unsaddle Prince and picket him so he wouldn't run off. It wasn't that I didn't trust him; he'd come like a puppy when I called him. I tied him because I didn't want him scared off by a cougar or some other wild critter that might wander by.

When Prince was contentedly chomping grass, I'd take my cartridges or fishing pole, depending on where I was, and my book and make myself comfortable. When I got tired of either fishing or shooting, I'd read for a while and then take a nap or, as the Mexicans call it, a *siesta*. When I woke up, I'd eat what I'd caught, shot or brought from home, after doing what cleaning and cooking was necessary. Then I'd read some more before heading back to the ranch and whatever chores I had to do.

Sometimes I got back to the ranch a little later than others because I had either slept longer or had come to a place in what I was reading that was so good I couldn't stop. And let me tell you, with the books Ma and Miss Ross gave me, there were plenty of good places! I read *The Last of the Mohicans, Oliver Twist, The Spy, Rob Roy* and some strange stories by a man named Edgar Allan Poe. I didn't always understand everything I read, but I got most of it, and what I got was good.

The morning after we got the letter from my grandparents, I made one of my trips to my fishing hole. I had caught three large catfish and two

trout that were keepers; then the fish stopped biting. I got out my book and read a story by Poe, "The Murders in the Rue Morgue." It was about a detective who solved a terrible murder mystery by finding clues that the police had missed. When I had finished the story, I laid the book aside and stretched out on the ground with my head on the saddle.

I woke up an hour or so later from a nightmare about a huge monkey chasing me with a straight razor. I shuddered and called, "Prince!" When I heard his answering whinny, I felt better. "Don't come, pardner," I said. "I just wanted to make sure that monkey hadn't scared you away."

I was hungry, and the thought of those fish cooking in my frying pan made my mouth water. From my saddlebags I got out the pan and the small coffeepot I always carried; then I gathered some dry brush and built a fire. When I walked to the edge of the water and stooped to get the piece of twine I had used for a stringer, I couldn't believe my eyes. It was gone! The stick I had shoved into the soft mud after I had tied the twine to it had been pulled up. It hadn't been dragged into the water by the fish; it had been pulled up by a human hand while I had been sleeping.

I looked around to see if anything else had been taken. I saw that my book was lying on a rock ten or twelve feet from where I had left it. Still looking around, I walked over and picked it up. A wrinkled scrap of paper was sticking out of the book, marking my place. Someone had scribbled this message on it in pencil:

Only the book-learning part of school is over for the summer. It's time for a lesson. I have your fish. Find me in time, and we'll eat them together.

There was no signature, but I knew the handwriting.

I put out my fire, collected everything and saddled Prince. I had a trail to find!

CHAPTER TWO

Before I mounted Prince, I circled the area slowly, looking for tracks. I had no idea how long ago the thief had stolen my fish, but I guessed he had made his move as soon as he was sure I was asleep. I must have been right because the grass that had been trampled under his feet had straightened back up, making it so I couldn't tell where he had walked.

I made a second, wider circle, watching the ground closely for anything that didn't look right. As I thought of "The Murders in the Rue Morgue," suddenly I became the famous French detective, C. Auguste Dupin.

"Mr. Dupin, we really need your help. You see, sir, some low-down, dirty, double-crossing polecat has stolen five fish that had 40,000 francs in gold hidden in them. He cut the rope with a straight razor and then lit a shuck for the border. Can you find him?"

Dupin looked at the dusty deputy for a moment, then replied, *"Oui, Monsieur,* I will take the case."

The great detective circled the camp once but found nothing. On the second time around, he widened the circle and moved more slowly.

"Aha!" he exclaimed suddenly as he picked up something from the grass with his thumb and forefinger and held it up for all to see. "Our clever thief has come this way. See, here is a cricket—dead but not dried out or eaten by ants. It died beneath a foot not long ago. He went this way."

For the next two hours the "detective" followed the cleverly hidden trail, sometimes on horseback, sometimes walking, sometimes even crawling on his hands and knees as he searched the ground for clues. Then the trail simply disappeared.

"Now what are we going to do, Mr. Dupin?" the deputy asked.

"Now," replied Dupin as he seated himself on a

nearby boulder and closed his eyes, "I am going to think." Five minutes later he opened his eyes and stood up. "But of course! I have him!"

The detective leaped onto the back of his fleet-footed pony, Prince, and galloped back toward camp. When he was within half a mile of his camp, the great Dupin slowed Prince to a walk. At a quarter of a mile away, he dismounted and tied Prince's reins to a small bush. Creeping quietly from bush to rock to tree, he stole toward the camp where he knew the thief would be. A slight breeze brought the smell of cooking fish to his nostrils. "Aha!" said the great detective. "I have him for sure!"

Silent as a snake, he wriggled forward until he was just a stone's throw from the campfire. The thief had not only opened up the fish and removed the forty thousand francs, he had cooked the fish and now sat eating them with his back to the detective! As the master detective planned the capture of this villain, the man took a drink from his coffee cup and spoke without turning his head.

"Now that you finally got here, you might as well come into camp and eat. I've cleaned these fish and cooked them, and they're mighty tasty. Coffee's good too."

I got to my feet, dusted off my pants and walked into camp. "Chad, how could you have known I was there? I didn't make a sound."

Chad grinned at me. "No, you didn't. I couldn't

have been quieter myself. A man just develops a sixth sense after a while, and he knows when he's being watched. Are you hungry?"

While we ate, Chad had me tell him in detail how I had followed his trail. When I had finished the tracking part and reached the point where the trail had disappeared, Chad grinned, but he was curious. "Never mind for right now how my trail disappeared. I want to know what brought you back here if you had no trail to follow."

"C. Auguste Dupin showed me the way," I replied.

"Who?" Chad asked, puzzled.

"A great French detective I brought with me this morning gave me some ideas. I tried them; I found you." As Chad looked around, I laughed. "Hold on, Chad; I met him in the book I'm reading. Listen to this."

Then I told Chad about another Dupin story called "The Purloined Letter." In it Dupin explained that he had learned from a boy how to figure out the way someone else would think: put yourself in his place and then act the way he would act.

"When I got to the place where your trail disappeared, I did what Dupin would have done," I explained. "I sat on a boulder, closed my eyes and pretended to be you. I knew you were trying to teach me to track, and I remembered that you're always telling me to track with my mind as well as with my senses. I knew you'd want to eat in a place where there was plenty of water for making coffee and for washing after cleaning the fish.

"Then I thought, *If I were in his place, I wouldn't want to be dragging those fish all over the territory because the smell would stay on my saddle for days.* That's when I figured that if I were you, I wouldn't have taken the fish far away; I'd have just moved them. I'd have left a trail leading away from here for a few miles, then doubled back and made myself at home in the best place around while the one tracking me looked all over for my trail. Am I right?"

Chad shook his head. "Who'd ever believe that there were books where people think like that? That Dupin feller must have been some kind of tracker. I believe he'd be a good man to ride the river with."

"I believe he would, Chad," I proudly replied.

Chad was reaching for the coffeepot when he suddenly froze. "Listen! There's a rider coming!" he whispered.

CHAPTER THREE

"Tell me what you see, pardner," Chad whispered.

Our breakfast temporarily forgotten, we both stood watching the trail of dust rise off the long, dry plain that approached the river for nearly a mile on both sides. "One rider...still too far away to make out," I began.

"What else? Quick!"

"Uh, something's different about his horse, and the rider is small—smaller than me, I reckon."

"What's different about the horse?" Chad asked.

They were getting close enough for me to see the rider leaning forward over the horse's neck; the wind caused the brim of the rider's hat to stand straight up. Something was different—and then I saw it. I turned to Chad, who was already grinning, and I said, "It's not a horse; it's a mule! That's Jasper coming. I recognize the way he rides, and he's still far enough away that if he was someone you either didn't know or didn't want to see, you could let him know or at least keep him covered."

Chad put his hand on my shoulder. "Pardner, you may live to be a cowboy yet! Now, if I know Jasper, he'll be starving; so if we want any more of this fish, we'd best get it on our plates right now!"

As we sat and watched Jasper ride toward us, we continued to eat the hot, delicious catch. Jasper was bouncing up and down in the saddle looking like a scarecrow that someone had tied to a mule. Although he was just over two years younger than me, he was one of my best friends. I liked him since the first time I had seen the "turtle head" at school, his fuzzy hair cut at different lengths and sticking out in all directions. With his slumped shoulders, skinny neck and large head, he had looked to me like a giant tortoise that had been pulled from its shell and trained to walk on its hind legs.

For a minute we thought Jasper was going to ride straight into the river, but he managed to stop that big mule about twenty feet from our fire. As he half slid, half fell off the right side of his mule, it laid its ears back, kicked at Jasper, then tried to bite him.

After tying the mule to a scrawny scrub oak, Jasper patted its neck and said softly to it, "Good boy, Jasper, good boy!"

Chad and I looked at each other, then Chad spoke: "Jasper, your mule's name is Jasper too?"

"Yep. I was riding not far from the house when I heard Ma calling, 'Jasper! Jasper!' I said to my mule, 'Well, I declare! Your name must be Jasper too!' That's what I've called him since then. He's a good mule except he don't like me getting on or off him."

"Jasper," I said, "that's probably because you're getting on and off from the right side. Horses and mules are broken to be mounted and dismounted from the left side."

Jasper looked puzzled for a minute, but then he looked at us through squinting eyes. "Oh, I get it," he said. "You reckon I'm so dumb that I can't tell my right from my left, don't you? Well, Mr. Arty the Smarty, I can," and Jasper the boy turned around facing Jasper the mule. "This is my left hand," he said, and he raised his left hand. "That means that this," and he patted the mule's right side, "is his left side."

"That's *right*," I began instructing him, "and you have to face the same—"

"I *know* it's right," he said, shaking his head, "so could we stop talking and eat the rest of the fish?"

I looked at Chad, but he just kinda shrugged his shoulders. "Sure," I said, "help yourself, and then tell us why you were in such a hurry."

Jasper scraped the rest of the fish from the frying pan onto a plate he had taken from his saddlebags. He walked over to the river, filled his tin cup, then sat down and put a large piece of fish in his mouth. He chewed for a minute, swallowed, then took a drink from his cup.

He was about to speak, but Chad headed him

off. He stood up, took a last sip of coffee and emptied his cup on the ground behind him. "Well, boys, I hate to miss the fun, but I have to ride. Your ma doesn't pay me to cook catfish, and your lesson from me is over for now. You two try to stay out of trouble. I'll be checking fence in the north quarter all day, so I'll probably get back about suppertime."

After washing his cup, frying pan and plate in the river, Chad shook them dry and put them into one of his saddlebags. Then he mounted his big bay gelding and rode off toward the north.

"Now, Jasper, what's your big news?" I asked.

Jasper's eyes bulged as he chewed a huge piece of fish he had just crammed into his mouth. He must have tried to swallow it too soon because he choked on it. I thumped his back, and he guzzled water until he had stopped coughing. He looked at me with watery eyes. "Thanks, Arty. I come out here to tell you I found something."

He grinned at me, stretching his long, skinny neck and looking more than ever like a turtle's head. Then he jumped to his feet and ran to his mule. With his back to me, he reached into his saddlebag. When he turned around, he was waving a pistol in my direction. "Reach for the sky or grab for your gun, you dirty sidewinder!"

I screamed and threw myself face down on the ground. "Don't point that thing at anyone, Jasper! It could go off!"

The grin left Jasper's face, and he let his arm

fall to his side so that the pistol aimed into the
ground. "I'm sorry, Arty," he said apologetically; "I
wasn't planning on pulling the trigger. I don't
even think it's loaded." He closed one eye and
lifted the gun, looking down the barrel.

"Jasper!" I yelled, jumping to my feet. "Give me
that gun!"

"No, it's mine! I found it!" he said, stepping
back and bumping into his cranky mule, which
tried to kick him.

"I just want to see it, Jasper. Come on."

His eyes narrowed. "Promise to give it back?"

"Promise," I said, holding out my hand.

The gun was the same size, weight and caliber

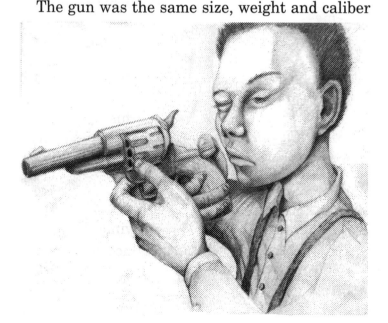

as mine, but the likeness ended there. This gun, instead of the usual blue-black finish, was a shiny silver color. Instead of plain, wooden grips on the handle, it had fancy white pearl grips. Five chambers of the cylinder were loaded; one was empty. Marshal Bodie had taught me to keep my own gun that way so that it couldn't accidentally go off while I was riding.

I looked at Jasper, who was still grinning. "You found this?" I asked.

"Yep," he replied, nodding his head.

"Where?"

Jasper took off his hat and ran his fingers through his uncontrollable, fur-like hair. "Well, Pa guv me—"

"Gave," I corrected.

"...*gave* me the day off from the store. He said he couldn't afford to keep me there all day. I told him I'd be with you either here or at the canyon where you shoot. I didn't know where you was—"

"*Were.* Oh, sorry, Jasper," I said, seeing the frustration in his face, "but you did ask me to help you with your speaking."

"I know, I know. You just make it plumb hard for a body to tell you anything when you keep interrupting like that. Now, where was I? Oh, yeah, I didn't know where you *were,* so I went to the canyon first. You wasn't...no...weren't there, so I started to leave, but I seen a—"

"*Saw,* Jasp—"

"Give me that gun, Arty," said Jasper, holding out one hand, "and next time you break in on me, so help me, I'll—"

"Wait!" I interrupted, hiding the pistol behind my back long enough to turn the cylinder and eject each of the bullets out on the ground behind me. "Here, you hold it. I promise not to interrupt you again."

Jasper continued: "There was a sparkle in the sunlight just inside the mouth of the canyon, so I rode down there; and there was this pistol, laying right there on the ground." He pretended to blow smoke off the opening of the pistol barrel. Then he used the barrel to push back the brim of his hat.

"Did you see anything else?" I asked.

Jasper looked at me, surprised. "Shucks, Arty, you've been there enough times. I saw brush and rocks and three horned toads and—"

"I mean anything unusual, Jasper, you..." I stopped myself. I knew that getting angry because Jasper wasn't talking fast enough to suit me wouldn't help either of us. I took a deep breath and tried again. "I mean, was there anything different around the canyon?"

Jasper pointed the gun at an imaginary target, holding it in both hands and moving it to follow the target's movement. "Bang! Bang!" Again he blew the imaginary smoke from the barrel, then grinned at me. "You know, I reckon the ground was a might tore up right around there, but after I seen...*saw* this here pistol, I wasn't noticing nothing else. Do you think I can keep it?"

"I don't know, Jasper," I said. "Let's head for the canyon and see if we can find out what happened to its owner. A man wouldn't leave this pistol lying on the ground and walk away from it without a good reason. Clean up your dishes, and then we'll ride!"

CHAPTER FOUR

Half an hour later, Jasper and I dismounted outside the mouth of Coyote Canyon. After Jasper had pointed out the place where he had found the gun, I left him with his mule and started circling about looking for signs, just like Chad had taught me. I repeated his words softly to myself: *The story's almost always there, if a man knows how to read it.*

When I suddenly turned around so that I could see things from a different angle, I found Jasper's face six inches from mine. We both screamed.

"Jasper," I said, trying to control myself, "didn't I ask you to stay with your mule?"

He looked blankly at me and then held up his right hand to show me the reins of his mule, which he had been leading behind him. "I did, Arty!"

There was nothing I could say. I pointed back toward the place where Prince was standing and said quietly, "Jasper, wait over there."

As I studied the area where he had found the pistol, several things were plain. A galloping horse had stumbled and fallen and then had gotten up again and had run into the canyon. The horse's rider had lost his pistol and either had not noticed or had not had the time to pick it up. Someone must have been chasing him. I made a wider circle and found another set of tracks leading toward the canyon. Ten minutes later I was certain there were no tracks leading out.

"Jasper," I whispered as soon as I was close enough to be heard. "Two sets of tracks lead into this canyon, and none come out. Coyote Canyon is a box canyon. Do you know what that means?"

Jasper looked thoughtful for a moment, bobbing his turtle head up and down. "Yep," he answered. "A box canyon has only a front door. There's no other way in or out. Anybody knows that."

"Jasper!" I said, trying hard to stay at a whisper. "It means there are still two people in Coyote Canyon, and one of them is missing a pistol."

Jasper's eyes bulged even more than usual. "What are we going to do?"

I looked at him and grinned. "I reckon we couldn't do any harm by looking around a little."

Jasper grinned back at me, and we climbed into our saddles. If we had known what we were getting into, we wouldn't have been so light-hearted.

As we walked our horses into the canyon, my throat was dry, my heart was pounding, and I was sweating enough to fill up the horse trough. I tried to watch the trail of the first horse and keep my eyes on the rocks around us at the same time. I had seen several dark stains on the rocks, dirt and weeds along the trail before I realized what they were.

Motioning for Jasper to stop, I dismounted, pried a small piece of stained rock from the ground and smelled it. The scent was weak, but it was there.

"What is it, Arty?" Jasper asked softly.

I looked up at him, feeling my stomach starting to knot. "Blood," I replied.

Back on Prince's back, I kept watching the rocks above us and the ground below us, but I also began to pay attention to Prince. Chad had taught me that a horse or a pony has far better hearing, sight and smell than most people have. Forty yards farther into the canyon, Prince began to snort and balk. Jasper's mule was acting the same way.

Because of the boulders and brush scattered all over the canyon, we couldn't see far in any direction. Still, I knew we were getting close to something. We tied our animals and continued on foot, both too scared to speak. With Jasper sticking to me like a shadow, I peeked around a boulder and saw a horse, only it wasn't standing. We didn't have to touch it to know that it was dead. The bullet wound in its head proved that. Also, a large gash in its side explained the blood on the trail and the reason its rider had shot it.

Jasper peeked over my shoulder but said nothing. Then his arm came up beside my face as he pointed to a sharp, jagged rock that looked like a giant arrowhead pointing toward the sky. "Look!"

he whispered. Sticking out from behind the base of the rock was a boot, its spur digging into the loose rock and its toe pointing toward the sky.

"I'm scared, Arty. Let's get out of here!"

"What if he's hurt and needs help?" I asked. "He could die before we got back. I'm just going to look. Wait here."

"No! I'm coming with you."

Together we worked our way over the smaller rocks and bushes and around the larger boulders until we had reached the pointed rock. I don't know what I expected to see, but what I saw was a man with blood all over his shirt and his eyes wide open, staring into the sun. We weren't going to be of any help to him.

"Let's go tell the marshal," I said.

As we turned to leave, I heard the unmistakable metallic click of a pistol being cocked. A cold, flat voice said quietly, "Now you boys just turn around nice and easy, and keep your hands where I can see them."

CHAPTER FIVE

As we turned slowly, Jasper and I faced each other for a second. Any other time I would have laughed at the look on his face, but nothing seemed very funny right then. A man stood there looking at us, a cocked gun in his left hand, and he wasn't laughing.

He was about six feet tall, lean and tough-looking. Something about him reminded me of a lobo wolf. The man had at least a week's growth of beard, and he was covered with dust from the top of his flat-crowned black hat to his worn, brown boots. He wore a blue-and-white-checked shirt, covered by a black leather vest, and black pants.

His blue eyes shifted from Jasper to me. He spoke in a raspy voice. "What are you boys doing out here? Drop those guns and then put your—hey, kid, give me that gun!"

After I had dropped my gun, he kicked it away from me, but then he grabbed the fancy gun from Jasper and stuck it in his own belt. While Jasper was explaining how he had found the gun, I was looking at the one the outlaw was holding. I reckon any gun looks big to the person on the business end of it, but this one really was big. It was two or three inches longer than mine and looked too heavy for a holster. Then I saw that the holster on his right hip already held a six-shooter the same size as mine.

"You should have minded your own business and not been so nosy," he growled.

Jasper and I both jumped as he suddenly placed the fingers of his right hand in his mouth and whistled. We heard the clatter of hooves on stone, and a dapple gray with a white blaze on his face appeared from behind a nearby boulder.

"I try not to shoot young'uns unless I have to," he warned. Grabbing the reins and swinging into the saddle, he slipped the huge revolver into a holster on his saddle. Crossing his hands on the pommel, he leaned forward to look at us. "But if either of you comes out of this canyon before an hour is up, I'm going to feel the need." Then the outlaw rode out of sight.

Both of us had been pretty scared, but I reckon curiosity had been keeping me from being more scared than I was. Something was bothering me, but I didn't know what.

Jasper walked up beside me. "What do we do now?" he asked.

"I'll tell you what we *don't* do," I replied. "We don't leave this canyon until we're sure an hour is up."

"How will we know?" he asked. "We don't have a pocket watch."

"Well," I said, "I guess we'll wait till we think we've waited an hour, and then we'll wait that much longer—just to be sure."

"What will we do while we wait?" Jasper asked as he took off his hat and wiped his sweaty face on his sleeve. "You can target practice, but he took my gun!"

At the mention of my gun, I realized that it was still in the dirt where the outlaw had kicked it. "I know what I'll do first," I said, looking at the dirty gun. Ten minutes later I spun the freshly cleaned cylinder and then holstered my gun. The whole time I was cleaning it, Jasper had sat on a rock, staring at the body that lay a few yards away.

Now, I had been to three or four funerals, not counting Pa's, where the coffin had been nailed shut as soon as the body was in it. I had seen dead people before, but they had been cleaned up and were peaceful looking. This man was neither.

I walked over to where the body was lying sprawled on the rocks. Getting close to him was hard to do for two reasons: one, being stuck out there in the canyon with a dead man just scared me; the other, Jasper had a handful of the back of my shirt and was stuck to me like my own shadow.

"Jasper!" I said, prying him away from me enough to turn around. "If you're that scared, go back and sit on the rock! You're going to trip me."

He backed off a little, and I squatted down by the body. I thought of Pa and wondered if this man

had been someone's husband or pa. I decided to
check his pockets. Maybe something there would
tell us who he was.

Twice I tried to touch the dead man's clothes,
but I couldn't. Then I remembered Detective
Dupin. By thinking the way he thought, maybe I
could succeed. Since the man was lying on his
back, I could reach into the pockets of his unbut-
toned leather vest without much trouble.

In his right pocket I found a tobacco pouch, cigarette papers and three short strips of jerked beef.
In his left pocket were five or six coins and a wad
of bills. I put the things in a small pile behind me.
His shirt had no pockets, but I knew that most
vests had an inside pocket. I swallowed hard and
carefully lifted the right side of the vest away
from the bloody shirt. There was no pocket. I took
a deep breath. With my right thumb and forefinger,
I slowly lifted the left side of the vest and found a
pocket. I carefully slid my left thumb and forefinger into the pocket.

"Could I have a piece of this jerky?" a voice
whispered in my ear.

Now, since I'm telling the story, I could say that
I calmly turned to Jasper and told him to take his
hand off my shoulder and go back and sit on his
rock; but I don't hold to lying, and no one would
believe a whopper like that anyway. I'm not sure
about the order they happened in or if it even mat-
ters. I just know that four things happened: I
screamed, jumped to my feet, lost my balance and

grabbed Jasper's shirt with one hand, then fell anyway, pulling Jasper down with me. We both landed right on top of that dead man.

If anyone had ridden by in the next few minutes and found two boys screaming and rolling around in the dust and rocks, he'd probably have thought we'd tangled with a bees' nest and were trying to get rid of them. I reckon we looked pretty funny, but I can tell you one thing: we weren't laughing.

Some time later Jasper was sitting on the rock again, and I was talking to him and holding the jerky in my hand. "You can't eat this," I said, trying to keep my voice from shaking.

"Why not?" Jasper asked, squinting the way he does when he is puzzled. "*He* sure ain't going to need it."

"It's evidence," I replied.

I walked back to the pile of the dead man's belongings and tried to become Dupin again. One good thing happened when we tangled with the dead body. As we fell across him, we knocked his vest open on his left side so that the pocket was easy to get at. There was a folded piece of paper sticking out of the pocket, but the thing that caught my eye was the badge pinned to the shirt. The dead man was a Texas Ranger!

I looked over my shoulder and found that Jasper had left his rock again and was sitting on the ground beside the pile of belongings. Squinting at me again, he asked, "Can't I have just a *little* piece of this evidence?"

I shook my head no, then pulled the paper from the vest pocket and unfolded it. It was a "Wanted" poster. Printed in large, black figures it read:

$1,000 REWARD
will be paid for the capture of
Scott Cooley
DEAD or ALIVE

Below this was a drawing of a man's face. He wore a hat and a full beard. The picture wasn't very good. It could have been anybody with a beard—even the Ranger. It didn't look like the outlaw; but then, he had had a shave in the last week or so.

Below the picture was a description:

Age, 29–32 years. Height, 5' 11". Weight, 180 pounds. Dark brown hair and beard, blue eyes, medium build. Wanted for the murders of Peter Border and Deputy Sheriff John Worley. Usually travels with three or four other unidentified riders.

"Jasper," I said, "come here a minute."

Jasper shuffled over to me, and I handed him the poster. I watched his lips move and his eyes get bigger as he read.

"This is evidence," I said. "Do you know what that means?"

"Yes," Jasper replied, handing the poster back to me and sighing. "It means I can't eat it."

Sometimes Jasper just made me want to run across the desert and scream at the top of my voice!

CHAPTER SIX

When I was sure more than an hour had gone by, we gathered the evidence, tied it in my bandanna and carried it to where we had left our mounts. Carefully, so as not to disturb the evidence any more than necessary, I placed the small bundle into one of my saddlebags. I had decided against leaving everything and going to fetch the marshal; someone might find the body and take anything that was worth something. And I sure wasn't going to ride for the marshal and leave Jasper alone with a dead body and edible evidence!

I forced myself to go back and check the dead Ranger's pants pockets, but all I found were an extra bandanna and a clasp knife. I was satisfied that we had taken all the important stuff to give to Marshal Bodie.

On the way back to town, I kept Jasper quiet by giving him some of the jerky I always carried in my saddlebags; I needed some quiet time to think. I knew I was just a kid with a good imagination and no experience in solving crimes. Still something didn't seem quite right, but no matter how hard I tried, I couldn't figure out what it was.

Now, Marshal Bodie was a United States marshal, not a town marshal. A town marshal only had authority in the town that had hired him. From what I had learned since moving to Texas, a town marshal usually served until he quit or someone shot him. But a United States marshal was appointed by the President and had authority over a large area—sometimes a whole state. He could hire as many deputies as he needed, but his interest was in cases that were federal offenses. Because of the large territory Marshal Bodie had to cover, there were times when he was gone for several days. When I slid off Prince and opened the marshal's door and found only an empty office, I reckoned this must be one of those times.

I followed Jasper across the street to the general store and waited until his father had finished filling an order for a cowboy I didn't know. As the cowboy walked out of the store, Mr. Wilson turned to us, smiled and asked, "What can I do for you two *hombres?*"

"Do we really look like bad men?" I asked.

"You look like bad *boys,*" he said, still smiling. "What have you been up to?"

Jasper opened his mouth to answer. Ma had always taught me to be polite, but I knew that if I let Jasper talk, we could wind up in big trouble. I just headed him off at the pass.

"We've been out at Coyote Canyon," I replied. "Have you seen the marshal today?"

"Yes," Mr. Wilson replied. "He was in here picking up a few things this morning. He said he was headed for your place this afternoon. If he wasn't in town when you rode in, you must have just missed him."

I thanked him and asked if Jasper could ride out to the ranch with me. I knew I couldn't leave him there to tell what had happened.

"Reckon as long as he's back by dark, I can spare him," said Mr. Wilson.

Before we left town, I bought Jasper and myself two peppermint sticks apiece. As much as I like peppermint sticks, I really bought them to keep Jasper quiet so I could think.

I had seen something that didn't seem right, but what was it? Solving a little mystery in order to catch Chad was a game, but what I was doing now was the real thing. The one thing that I knew for sure was that I didn't know anything for sure.

We rode slowly, and Jasper kept stopping to chase horned toads and scorpions and even jackrabbits. Each time he mounted or dismounted his mule, it tried to bite him or kick him. In spite of the fact that I laughed at him, I was afraid that sooner or later he wouldn't get out of the way in time.

"Jasper," I said after watching another close call, "come here." I dismounted and stood beside Prince. "Stand beside your mule like I'm standing beside Prince," I said. "Now, raise your left hand."

"Didn't we already do this?" he asked.

I could tell he was beginning to get a little angry with me, but I still couldn't stop myself from grinning.

"I know the difference between right and left!" he said. "I'll prove it. You wear your gun on the right side, and Chad wears his on the left—like the dead man."

I kept showing him which side to mount and dismount, and fifteen minutes later I stood and watched proudly as Jasper mounted his mule from the left side. He spoke from the saddle: "He likes it! All this time he's been biting and kicking because he didn't know his right from his left! Thanks, Arty!"

I didn't stop grinning until we dismounted in front of the ranch house. The timing was perfect. Before we got to the door, it opened and Marshal Bodie came out. I was glad we were outside because I didn't exactly want Ma to hear what I had to tell him. I was pretty sure she wouldn't understand why we hadn't gone straight to the marshal in the first place.

Marshal Bodie didn't exactly understand either.

CHAPTER SEVEN

We walked away from the house so Ma wouldn't hear us. Marshal Bodie said nothing while I told him what had happened. "I reckon that's about it, Marshal," I said.

He took off his Stetson and laid it on the gatepost to our main corral. Untying his bandanna from his neck, he wiped his face with it, then retied it. As he replaced his hat, I had a fearsome

picture in my head: I was hog-tied so I couldn't
move. Close beside me on the ground was a bundle of five sticks of dynamite. The fuse was burned
nearly to the bundle.

"You reckon that's about it?" Marshal Bodie
asked quietly.

The fuse was now an inch long. I braced myself
for the explosion.

Facing me, the marshal put one hand on each
of my shoulders. I looked him in the eye as he
began to speak.

"Son, you know that you and Jasper could have
been killed, but I understand that you knew someone might be in trouble. You had to make a call
that could have meant life or death to a rider in
trouble. If I had been that rider, I'd have been
mighty glad to see you."

"You mean you're not riled at me?" I asked.

"I mean I'm proud of you, Arty. This isn't anything like that stunt you pulled with Phantom
awhile back." The fuse fizzled out.

The Marshal rubbed the back of his neck with
one hand and shook his head. "Arty, I understand
why you did what you did. I'm just wondering if
your ma will." The fuse was burning again.

"You're going to tell Ma?" I asked. There was a
knot in my stomach. Marshal Bodie looked as if
he'd seen my bundle of dynamite.

"Not me, pardner!" he said, raising his hands
with the palms toward me. "You have to bust your

own broncs. I'm just saying that *I'm* not the one who should be doing the telling. What do you think?"

Someone added another stick of dynamite to the bundle. "I think if Ma finds out from me, she might be pretty angry with me," I said, "but if she finds out from someone else, I'm buzzard bait."

Marshal Bodie smiled at me. "You know what James 4:17 says, 'To him that knoweth to do good, and doeth it not, to him it is sin.' I'm trusting you to do the right thing."

Jasper and I watched Marshal Bodie ride off toward Coyote Canyon. Jasper had been sitting in a rocking chair on our front porch while the marshal and I were talking. He had finished his second peppermint stick and was licking his sticky fingers.

"Why is the marshal going that way?" he asked. "Town is the other way."

"He's going to Coyote Canyon," I answered.

"No!" Jasper yelled, jumping from his chair, his eyes bulging. He looked around to be sure we were alone. "Arty," he whispered, "that's where the dead Ranger is. Marshal Bodie will find him!"

"Jasper," I whispered back, "that's why he's going. I told him everything."

Jasper scowled. "That ain't fair, Arty! I want to tell…" He grinned at me, a gleam in his eyes. "My turn—I get to tell your ma!"

I caught the collar of his shirt and stopped him just as he reached the front door. "Hold on there, pardner!" I said, still whispering. "We can't tell

Ma just yet. Marshal Bodie, you and I are the only ones who know what happened out there. For now, we need to keep it that way."

He looked like he was about to cry. "But I have to tell someone or I'll bust."

I knew he was telling the truth. I thought hard for a minute. All of a sudden I had an idea. "I'll tell you what," I whispered. "You have to get back to town. On the way, if you keep your voice down, you can tell your mule the whole story."

Jasper folded his arms across his chest and squinted at me. "You must think I'm pretty stupid."

"Why?" I asked, trying my best to look innocent.

"Because as soon as I leave, you'll tell Prince. Then you'll have told the story *twice,* but I'll only get to tell it once."

I put my arm around Jasper's shoulder. "You know, I hadn't thought of that; but you're right. I want to be fair because we're pardners. I'll tell you what. Before you ride back to town, let's you and me go out to the corral. We'll get Prince off in a corner where the other horses can't hear, and we'll tell him together. Then everything will be even."

Jasper's eyes bulged, and he grinned at me. "Let's go, *par-do-ner!*"

CHAPTER EIGHT

"Artemus, what's bothering you?" Ma asked. Too late I realized that I had just been playing with my food. Ma usually had to tell me once during each meal to slow down. When she finished eating before I did, she knew something had to be wrong.

I tried to think of something truthful that wouldn't get me in trouble.

Before I could say anything, Ma reached across the table and put her hand on mine. "I know what's bothering you," she said quietly.

I jumped, pulling my hand from under hers so fast that I almost knocked my plate into my lap. I could see in my mind a mountain of dynamite ready to explode. "You do?" I asked.

"I'm worried about your grandparents too, but they'll be all right. God will protect them the same way He protected us when we came out here," she assured me.

Finding that body in Coyote Canyon had made me forget everything else, so Ma's last sentence rattled my brain. Finally I understood what she was talking about. I made myself smile, and I reached out to hold her hand. A flash flood was washing away that mountain of dynamite.

"I'm sure God will keep them safe, Ma."

Usually I was asleep a few minutes after I went to bed. That night I was still awake after midnight. Finally I got out of bed and lit a lamp. Something was still nagging at me. Something I had seen or heard during the day hadn't been right, but I didn't know what that something was.

"God," I prayed, "You know what I'm missing. It might be something that will help Marshal Bodie catch a killer. Please help me remember what it is."

A voice inside me said, *Tell your ma about what happened.*

"I will, God," I whispered. "I'll tell her tomorrow."

Sitting on the edge of my bed with my head in my hands, I started backtracking the day, beginning at the point when Jasper and I had ridden into Coyote Canyon. I thought about every word, every move of Jasper, the outlaw and me.

Suddenly, there it was! I stood up, and so did the hair on the back of my neck. In my mind I was back in Coyote Canyon, standing face-to-face with the outlaw, and I could see him as clearly as before, but now I wasn't quite so scared. I also remembered something Jasper had said when we stopped on the way home so I could teach him how to mount his mule. *"You wear your gun on the right side, and Chad wears his on the left—like the dead man."*

The outlaw had worn a holstered gun on his *right* hip, but he was holding the big pistol in his *left* hand. He had stuck the fancy pistol in his belt with the butt facing the *left* side. The dead man's holster was on the left side. Why would a left-handed man keep his tobacco, papers and jerky in his *right* pocket? I had never known a cowboy to do that.

I knew I needed to tell Marshal Bodie that something was wrong. I knew I should ride into town first thing in the morning. I also knew I wasn't going to be able to go to sleep.

Fifteen minutes later I had written Ma a note, telling her I had gone to town early. I had left it on the table and sneaked out of the house. After saddling Prince, I was riding toward town. You'd think someone who knew so much would be a smart man, but I reckon at that moment I wasn't so smart.

Probably I wouldn't have gone had the night been real dark, but the moon was bright— brighter than I was, at least.

I was hoping that one of two things would happen. I might talk to the marshal and be back home before sunup; then I could tear up the note I had left and be back in my bed when Ma got up. If that didn't happen, Ma might find the note when she got up and figure I had just left; then she wouldn't be worried about me. After all, I hadn't said *how* early I was riding to town.

Letting Prince go at his own pace, I tried to sort out some things. Why would the outlaw want to take the Ranger's gun? Because an extra gun was always a good thing to have. From the stories I'd heard, I knew that a gun might get jammed, broken or even lost. Most of the hands had a spare six-gun somewhere.

What made no sense to me was why the outlaw had traded holsters with the dead man. Why would he go to the trouble of buckling his own holster to the Ranger's waist? Marshal Bodie would have to figure out that mystery.

White Rock looked like a ghost town in the moonlight. The only things stirring were three coyotes and a dozen or more jackrabbits I had seen as I was riding in. As I rode up the wide, dusty street toward the marshal's office, I saw no sign of life. Light was coming from a few windows, but only the tumbleweeds moved in the wind.

I tied Prince to the hitching rail in front of the marshal's office. I knew he had a room at the hotel, but I didn't want to be caught wandering through the hotel in the middle of the night. Sometime during the night Marshal Bodie made his rounds—walking through town to be sure everything was all right. I was hoping he hadn't made them yet. I planned to wait in front of the jail until he came.

As I stepped onto the wooden sidewalk, I saw light in the cracks between the closed shutters. Quietly I stepped to the door and put my ear against it. Holding my breath, I heard voices from inside, but they must have been almost whispering because I couldn't make out the words. I was sure that one voice was the marshal's, but I didn't recognize the other one. Before I knocked on the door, I wanted to know who was inside.

One side of the marshal's office was attached to the funeral parlor. The other side had a small window that faced the livery stable, which stood some yards away. Quietly I sneaked around to that window. The shutter there was closed too, but when I put my eye to the crack, I saw Marshal Bodie, with his back to me, sitting on his desk and talking to the other man. The stranger must have been sitting in the old chair in the corner because I couldn't see him through the crack.

Just for a minute the wind died, and I could make out some of what they were saying. "You'll need this," said Marshal Bodie. He was holding a gunbelt and holster.

"Thanks, Luke," replied the stranger. "I think I have everything I need for now. I'll get the rest when it's safe to come back. In the meantime, I'll…" The wind picked up again, and I couldn't hear the rest of what he said. The stranger stood up and walked to the marshal's desk. When I saw his face, I shoved my bandanna into my mouth to keep from screaming. My knees gave out, and I sat down hard on the ground.

This time he had a smile on his face instead of a frown, and his face was in dim lamplight instead of bright sunshine. Still I had no trouble recognizing the outlaw who had killed the Ranger!

CHAPTER NINE

I just sat there on the ground with my back against the wall. What I had just seen and heard made no sense! I reckoned I'd wake up soon and find myself in my bed and Prince still in his stall.

But if this wasn't a nightmare and if the outlaw came out of the marshal's office, he'd run right into Prince. I crawled to the corner and peeked around it. Prince stood looking at me. He snorted softly.

"Easy, boy! Quiet, Prince," I whispered. I walked as quickly as I could to him, stroked his face and spoke softly to him while untying his reins from the hitching rail. Holding my breath, I led him around the corner to the alley where I'd been standing.

The door to the marshal's office opened and closed. I was close enough to hear boots hit the wooden sidewalk and then the dusty street. I waited until the jingle of spurs faded away before letting out my breath. Taking off my hat, I peeked around the corner. I could see the marshal walking toward the hotel. Putting my eye to the crack, I saw only a dark room. I took a deep breath and let it back out slowly.

"That was a close one!" I whispered to Prince. Then those short hairs on the back of my neck stood up, and I felt cold. I thought about the time I had been hunting a cougar and wound up being hunted by him. I knew where the outlaw *wasn't,* but I didn't know where he *was.* I was pretty sure he had gone out the back door. What I had to find out was where he had gone next.

Leading Prince, I started toward the back corner of the building. After taking only one or two steps, I heard the sound of hoofbeats. A horse was trotting along behind the marshal's office heading for the other end of town. I listened until there was only the sound of the wind. I was safe!

Now, what most folks would expect to happen next would be that I jumped on Prince and lit a shuck for home, and I was planning to do just that. I would ride back to the ranch, tell Ma everything, and we would figure out what to do. Then she would take away my gun, Prince, my hat, my boots and would send me into the desert with no canteen, where the buzzards would get me. I still should have lit a shuck for home, but I didn't; instead, I got curious. I wondered if the back door to the undertaker's shop was locked. It was, but the window wasn't; in fact, it was wide open. It wasn't a big window, but I'm not a big boy.

I knew it was wrong, but I crawled through that window and into the blackest darkness I'd ever seen; but like the great detective, I had anticipated the problem and had taken a stubby candle and some matches from my saddlebag before crawling through the window. I didn't know what that back room looked like in daylight, but I can tell you, it was spooky by candlelight!

The room was small and shut off from the rest of the building by a closed door. The only furniture was a heavy wooden table in the middle of the room—and on it was a coffin! I took a deep breath, raised the candle and walked to the table. He'd been cleaned up a bit, but the body in the coffin was the Ranger.

I reckoned no one on the street would be able to see a light in that room, so I lit a lamp, then blew out my candle. I set the lamp on a shelf above the coffin and looked around. There were two other

coffins leaning against the back wall. I hoped they were empty. In one corner was an open keg of nails with the handle of a hammer sticking out.

On the floor beside the nail keg was what first looked to me like a pile of rags. When I stepped closer and saw the dark stains, I knew I was looking at the dead Ranger's clothes. I turned back to the coffin. Someone—I reckoned Mr. Talbot, the undertaker—had washed the Ranger's face and combed his hair. A white sheet covered the body, toes to neck.

Some folks might say I was loco, but for half of the gold in Texas—and I couldn't tell you why—I wanted to touch that dead man. So I reached out with my trigger finger and held my breath.

Now, when a person is scared, timing is everything. If that owl had flown past the window and screeched one minute earlier or one minute later, I would have been fine. But he didn't, and I wasn't. Just as my finger passed the top of the sheet, that owl cut loose.

I tried to scream, but all I did was suck air. I kept breathing in through my wide-open mouth. I tried to push some air out again, but I just couldn't make it happen. After I had finally breathed out two or three times, I was ready to leave. My curiosity about touching that dead body could wait a spell.

I wanted to leave things the way I had found them. My finger had caught hold of that sheet when I jerked my hand back, and the sheet was down halfway to the man's waist. I needed to pull it back up to his chin. Pinching the edge of the sheet between the thumb and trigger finger of each hand, I started to pull.

Then I saw the wound.

I'm not talking about the wound that had killed the Ranger; the sheet hadn't come down far enough to uncover that one. This wound was small and on the Ranger's left chest muscle. There were two small holes less than an inch apart. Once before, I had seen something that looked like this. One of the ranch hands had been bitten by a rattlesnake just above the top of his boot. The marks had been bigger and a little farther apart, but they were like the ones I was now staring at.

I pulled the sheet up the rest of the way and shuddered—I had just tucked in a dead man for the night!

I blew out the lamp and put it back where I'd found it. Then I crawled through the window and mounted Prince. The moon had gone behind the clouds, but I knew he could find his way home. I thought I could get back to the ranch, take care of Prince and sneak back into the house well before daylight. I could sleep a little later than usual—if I could sleep at all. Too many things didn't make sense.

I meant to try to sort out some things on my way home, but I reckon I was just too tired. Prince was taking his time, and the easy motion of his gait rocked me to sleep. The next thing I knew, Prince was standing still. Holding my breath, I opened one eye. Prince was standing by the corral gate. I reckon he was waiting for me to dismount, take off his saddle and put him in the corral.

I was still pretty foggy with sleep when I closed the corral gate and started toward the house. What I saw then made me wake up in a hurry. The ranch house should have been dark, but there were lights everywhere. I was sure Ma must have found my note and been worried.

Then I saw it! Halfway between the ranch house and the bunkhouse was a huge Conestoga wagon. I stood still, listening to the canvas top rustling in the wind.

"Grandma and Grandpa!" I whispered.

CHAPTER TEN

I couldn't believe my eyes! I started to run for the ranch house. Then I stopped. The excitement drained out of me like coffee from a cup with a hole in its bottom. Sure, I was excited about seeing my grandparents, and I knew they would be excited to see me too. The problem was, they would be expecting to see me come through the door of my bedroom in my long johns with my hair all messed up. Now I was about to bust through the front door fully dressed and covered with dust. *"Be sure your sin will you find out"* raced through my head.

"Dear Lord," I prayed, "please give me at least half the sense of Jasper's mule!"

I had a plan. Keeping away from the light of the windows, I sneaked to the back of the house. My window wasn't locked, but it was closed. I knew I had to be quiet, and the window was noisy.

Ten minutes later I was in my room, pulling off my clothes and hoping that no one had heard me sneaking in. I messed up my hair and opened the door to my room.

There were hugs and kisses and plenty of talk

about what a fine young man I had become. There was talk also of kinfolk—some I could remember; others I'd never heard of before. Before I knew it, the sun was up. Grandma wouldn't hear of sitting down while someone else fixed breakfast, or "vittles" as she called it.

While Ma and Grandma were working on breakfast, Grandpa leaned back in the rocking chair, put his sock feet on an old footstool, folded his hands behind his head and looked at me through gold-rimmed spectacles. He yawned, then said, "We aren't in the habit of traveling at night, Arty, but when the rancher east of here told us how close we were to the Flying A, we decided to keep pushing until we got here." He yawned again and stretched.

"I'm glad we kept moving, but I declare, I don't know how long I'll be able to stay awake after breakfast. You must be tired too, eh?"

"Yes sir," I replied. "I can hardly keep my..." I sat up straight in my chair and looked at Grandpa. "How did you know I...I mean...what are you talking about?"

He took a folded piece of paper from his vest pocket. "I just happened to notice this before your ma did. While your ma and grandma were saying their howdies, I read your note. I thought that two o'clock in the morning was a little early for a boy your age to be going to town, so I—"

"Does Ma know?" I interrupted. I was starting

to feel a knot in my stomach.

"Know what?" asked Grandpa.

"That I was gone," I replied.

"I don't think so. I wandered over and peeked into your room while they were talking. I wanted to be sure you weren't in your bed."

"Are you going to tell her?" The knot was getting bigger.

"Well," said Grandpa, "I'd kind of like to hear what exactly you were up to before I make any decision about telling anybody anything. I'd like to—"

"Come and get it!" said Grandma.

Grandpa grinned and winked at me. "Call me anything you want, but don't call me late for breakfast. Let's eat, boy!"

After breakfast Ma said, "Arty and I will clear and wash. You two must be ready for a nap."

"I never could sleep during daylight hours," answered Grandma. "Let's get rid of these men, and I'll help you."

Grandpa pushed back his chair and said, "I'd like to have a look at this ranch of yours, if you have an extra horse and a man you can spare to show me around."

"We have plenty of extra horses," Ma said. Then she looked thoughtful. "But I don't know about an extra man to show you around."

"Ma!" I said.

She laughed, then said, "I'll send my top hand

with you if you two promise to keep out of trouble."

Grandpa winked at me and said to Ma, "We'll do our best. Don't expect us back until time for supper!"

Grandpa picked out and saddled Sally, a roan mare that was gentle but strong, and we spent the morning looking over the herd and the grazing land. Grandpa repaired a break in the fence, and we found buzzards feeding on four dead steers in the corner of the north pasture.

"Lightning hit them," Grandpa said after he had dismounted and looked at them closely. I was glad to ride away from that place with its awful smell.

We rode for another hour or so until we came to

a small spring. There was a little grass around a small basin of water. Two tall cottonwood trees made a shady spot large enough for a dozen head of cattle.

"What do you say to taking a siesta for a couple of hours? I'm really tired, and this looks like a good place to rest."

"I say yes, but how will we know when to wake up? I'm so tired I could sleep until sunup."

"Don't worry," Grandpa said. "I'll wake you in two hours." He pulled out his watch. "Half past ten," he announced.

We stretched out on the ground, using our blankets for pillows. I reckon I was really tired.

The next thing I knew, Grandpa was shaking me gently. "Nap time is over, boy. Let's ride."

I was feeling pretty good as we rode toward Coyote Canyon. "What time is it?" I asked.

Grandpa pulled out his watch and looked at it. "Quarter till one." He snapped its cover shut and returned the watch to his pocket.

I was surprised. "You must have slept exactly two hours, and then you woke up. How did you do it?"

"I can't say that I know for certain. I only know that if I go to sleep thinking about when I want to wake up, I wake up at that time. I've been that way since I was your age."

Before I could say anything further, his mood

changed, and he became quite serious. He spoke again. "Speaking of going to sleep and waking up, can you tell me about last night?"

"It was a beautiful night," I said. "There was a full moon, and you could see the stars—"

"Arty, you know what I mean."

"Yes sir," I replied. As we rode along, I told him everything, starting with Jasper's finding the gun and ending with my climbing through my bedroom window. The whole time I was talking, Grandpa said nothing. When I finished my story, we rode without talking until we got to Coyote Canyon.

"Show me where you found the body, Arty." When we got to the place, he dismounted, sat on a rock and said, "Let's talk."

CHAPTER ELEVEN

"Something is wrong, sure as shootin'," said Grandpa. "You're sure this Marshal Bodie is what he appears to be?"

"Yes," I replied, "and Ma trusts him too."

Grandpa sat there for a minute, just looking around. Then he pulled a big, blue bandanna from his back pocket, took off his broad-brimmed, tan hat and wiped his forehead and the back of his neck. He put his hat back on and began to fold the bandanna. "Your mother has always been a good judge of people," he said, looking across the canyon. "If both of you trust him, he must be a pretty good fellow."

He then looked at me and said, "Tell me again about the dead man."

When I had finished, Grandpa sat there for a few minutes without talking. Finally he asked, "Is that all? Are you sure you haven't forgotten anything?"

I closed my eyes and visualized the scene again. *Jasper and I were looking at the body. The outlaw surprised us, then left. I was going through the Ranger's pockets. Jasper scared me, and we fell on top of the dead ranger.*

"His face!" I said, jumping to my feet so quickly I scared Grandpa.

"Easy, boy." He put his hand on my shoulder. "Sit down and tell me about his face."

"It was two colors! I guess I was too scared to think about it until now. I didn't notice it in the dark room last night, but I noticed it in the sunlight."

"Take a deep breath and slow down, Son. What do you mean, two colors? Was he wearing war paint?"

"No," I answered, trying to slow down but not doing a very good job. "Most of his face was brown like mine, but his upper lip and chin were almost white. So was the lower part of his cheek from his mouth to his ear—at least on the side I saw."

"Which side was that?" asked Grandpa.

"The right side."

Somewhere in the back of my confused head, a door swung open, and a memory fell out on the floor. I reckon Grandpa must have seen something in my face.

"There's more, isn't there?" he prodded.

"What time is it?" I asked.

Grandpa looked surprised, but he reached into his right vest pocket with his right hand and took out his watch. "It's half-past one," he said, looking at his watch. "Why?"

He watched me through his spectacles while I told him about the dead Ranger's holster being on the left side while his tobacco and papers were on the right. I also told him about the outlaw holding his gun in his left hand and sticking the fancy gun in his belt so its butt faced the left side.

When I finished, Grandpa raised his eyebrows and whistled softly. "And then the marshal gave the dead man's gun belt and holster to the outlaw?"

"I saw him do it!" I replied.

"Well, if that don't beat all!" said Grandpa, shaking his head. "We need to do us some serious thinking." He stood and stretched with his hands on his lower back. "But this is not the kind of place where serious thinking can be done."

"What kind of place do we need?" I asked.

I held my breath and watched Grandpa rub his chin and look around. Finally he looked at me and winked. "We need us a fishing hole."

An hour later if someone had ridden past my fishing hole, he'd have found Grandpa and me doing just fine. He'd never have guessed by looking at us that we were hard at work solving a crime, but that's just what we were doing—part of the time.

We had to stop now and then to take a fish off the hook or put bait on a hook. I was sitting on the ground, leaning back on one elbow. Grandpa was sitting on an old blanket we'd brought, leaning against the trunk of a cottonwood tree. His hat was tilted forward so that I couldn't see his eyes. I think he was asleep for a while after the fish stopped biting.

I was almost asleep myself when Grandpa leaned forward and straightened his hat. "We're in over our heads, boy."

"What do you mean?" I asked. "You're not giving up, are you?"

"I reckon this crime is too complicated for us to figure out on our own," he replied. "Do you have the answers?"

"I haven't even figured out all the questions!"

"Well," he said with a grin, "I think we may be getting somewhere."

"Where?" I asked.

"Suppose you tell me." He grinned, tipped his hat forward again and leaned back against the tree.

"Grandpa!" I said, rolling onto my stomach and resting my chin in both hands. "How can I tell you what I don't know?"

"And how can I tell you what I don't know?" he asked. "What do we need here?"

"Help!" I answered.

"Now, where in the world are we going to get help?" he asked.

"I don't know. Even Dupin would be stuck on this one."

"Is that where your help usually comes from?" asked Grandpa.

One of those little doors in the back of my head opened again. This time a Bible verse fell out, and I said, "My help cometh from the LORD, which made heaven and earth!"

"Psalm 121, isn't it?"

"Verse two," I replied.

Grandpa leaned forward, took off his hat and laid it in his lap. "I think we'd better ask for some help then. Have at it, Arty."

I took off my Stetson, bowed my head and prayed: "My Father, I've done it again. I've been trying to do something on my own without including You. Please forgive me for riding on my own. Thanks for giving me a grandpa who has reminded me to ask for Your help. If You want us to solve this mystery, please show us the right trail to follow. Amen."

"Amen," said Grandpa, wiping his eyes with his bandanna. "Now, let's back off and take another run at this problem. Do you have a pocketknife?"

"No sir. But what does that—"

"You do now," he said, pulling something from his left vest pocket and tossing it to me. "I brought one for you. It's just like mine and just as sharp, so be careful."

"Thanks, Grandpa!" I looked at the knife in my hand and then at Grandpa. He was leaning against the tree again, his hat pulled down over his eyes. Then I looked at the knife. It was between three and four inches long with dark wood on both sides. I unfolded a shiny blade and grinned. Before I could say anything else, Grandpa spoke. "See if you can find a twig about as big around as your little finger and sharpen one end of it."

I found the twig with no trouble and began to sharpen one end. I also began to wonder if Grandpa was playing a joke on me or if he might have had a little too much sun. "Now what?" I asked.

"Now," said Grandpa, sitting up again, "we do a little experiment. Can you get me a piece of one of those little flat cacti that seem to grow everywhere out here?"

"Prickly pear?" I asked.

"Yep, I believe I have heard it called that—and scrape off all the spines so it's smooth."

I didn't have to go very far from the river to find one. Carefully I pulled off one of the sections that was a little bigger than my hand and used the knife to scrape away the spines while I walked back to Grandpa. Taking it between his thumb and trigger finger, he looked at both sides, then raised his eyebrows and looked at me. "Looks like somebody crossed a pickle with a pancake, doesn't it?" he said, grinning.

I grinned back at him. "Yep!"

"Now, let me borrow your pointed stick for a minute." He took the stick in his left hand and the piece of cactus in the palm of his right. After poking the point of the stick into the cactus, he pushed it along under the surface and then back through again, being careful not to poke through the back side. Then he handed it to me.

I turned it over in my hands, looking at it from every angle. If I had found it lying on the ground, I'd have thought that some little brave had been shooting his little bow and arrow at a cactus and this arrow had all but missed, just catching enough of the flat surface to hold it there.

"Pull the stick out and look at the holes it leaves," said Grandpa.

I obeyed. Grandpa said nothing. I knew he was waiting for me to discover something. I was afraid he'd be disappointed if I told him how happy I was that the little brave had found his arrow. I thought about everything we had talked about;

cactus hadn't even been mentioned.

Then I saw it. I looked at Grandpa, and he grinned. "It looks like the wound in the dead Ranger, only this is bigger!" I said.

"And green," he added. "You've seen the wound, but I haven't—"

"Then how did you know what it looked like?" I asked. "You know what made that wound, don't you? What was it?"

"Whoa, boy!" answered Grandpa. "I guessed, and I believe I'm right. Just to be sure, though, you study it a spell and see what you come up with."

I sat cross-legged on the ground and looked at the cactus and the stick. "The wound was a lot smaller than this one. That means that whatever made the hole was smaller—probably about the size of one of Ma's sewing needles. Now, how would a man come to stick himself with a sewing needle here?"

I held the cactus in my left hand and put my right hand over my heart. I pictured the dead Ranger in the canyon and then in the undertaker's room. Then I knew. "A badge!" I jumped to my feet. "Nobody wounded him. He stuck himself with his badge!"

"Must've been a pretty tough man," Grandpa said unexcitedly. "I expect that pinning a badge through your own skin would smart some, maybe enough when it went in one side to stop you from pushing it out the other."

I sat down again. "Grandpa, I've remembered everything I can that I saw in the canyon and at the undertaker's, but there must be something else there that I'm not seeing."

"What would your friend Dupin do?" asked Grandpa.

"I don't think he could do any better than I have. What could he see that I haven't seen?"

"Probably nothing," said Grandpa.

"So I'm in a box canyon. I have no place to go from here!"

"Before you ride out of that box canyon, Son, scout around one more time. Then tell me what you *don't* see. Sometimes what's missing will tell you as much as what's there."

He waved a fly away from his face and pulled the brim of his hat over his eyes again. As he leaned against the trunk of the tree, I could still see his mouth. He was smiling.

I was still holding the cactus in my left hand. Holding both hands in front of me, I studied them, trying to picture the dead Ranger's wound in the palm of my right hand. Then I started comparing the two wounds.

They looked alike except for color and size. Somehow I knew that I was right about the cause of the wound. Grandpa was right though—what kind of man would feel the pain of the pinpoint and keep pushing? A drunk maybe?

Still holding my hands side by side, I raised

them until they were right in front of my face. I watched a drop of clear juice ooze from one of the holes in the cactus, run onto the heel of my hand and start down my wrist.

It was Arty the Kid, not Dupin, who lowered his hands and spoke to his sidekick. "There wasn't any blood."

Grandpa pushed his hat back. "The undertaker would have washed it off," said he.

I was ready for that argument. "There was none the first time we saw the body either."

"Son, you've got the makings of a range detective. How do you account for this strange situation?"

"Grandpa, the only idea I have is a dumb one."

"Let's hear it. Sometimes if a fellow talks through a problem, things have a way of coming together even if he's talking to himself."

"All right," I said, "but I reckon you're going to laugh...and I don't blame you."

I had done plenty of things in my life that had made me feel dumb, but I didn't usually plan them ahead of time. I took a deap breath, then let it out slowly: "It's likely someone pinned that Ranger's badge on him *after* he was dead."

I closed my eyes and listened for Grandpa's laugh. When I didn't hear anything, I peeped at him through my right eye. Grandpa was watching me. "My thoughts exactly," he said.

"But, Grandpa, that doesn't make any sense!"

"You hit the nail on the head, Arty!" With that twinkle in his eye, I knew he was excited. I also knew that I was confused.

CHAPTER TWELVE

We rode toward the ranch slowly, side by side. Grandpa was quiet. Sometimes I talked to myself and sometimes to him. I was still stuck in a box canyon of confusion. "What am I missing, Grandpa?"

"Tell me the facts, one at a time," he said, smiling again.

"The Ranger is dead."

"Is he?" asked Grandpa.

"Of course!" I answered.

"How do you know?"

I was a little surprised that Grandpa would ask such a dumb question, but I answered, "Well, he'd been shot through the body. He wasn't moving or breathing. He—"

"I mean, how do you know the dead man was a Ranger?"

"He was wearing a badge..."

Before I finished, he asked, "But what other evidence do you have?"

With a gentle pull on the reins, I stopped Prince. Grandpa stopped Sally too, and I looked at him. "None," was my answer. That door in the back of my brain opened again, and ideas began to jump through it. "The badge was pinned through the man's skin, but there wasn't any blood on his shirt or vest."

"Why not?" asked Grandpa.

"Because...someone pinned it on him *after* he was dead!"

"Now why would a fellow want to do a thing like that?" Grandpa asked, tapping Sally's sides with his heels. Prince walked beside her without being told.

"I don't know," I answered.

"Just suppose the dead man wasn't a Ranger. Now then, take another look at your facts," said Grandpa.

"If he wasn't a Ranger," I stated, "then the out-law—I mean the other man—must be. Marshal Bodie's talking to a Texas Ranger would make sense, but why would they meet in the middle of the night and be sneaking around?"

"Good question," Grandpa replied. "We need to consider the dead man's face, the marshal's giving the dead man's gun to the stranger, the reward poster—"

"The reward poster?" I asked. "Why is that important?"

"I don't know," said Grandpa. "Maybe it isn't, but I don't think we should ignore it."

We didn't say much for the next half hour. I was praying and thinking, and I knew Grandpa was too. We let the horses run for a while, and then Grandpa had a few questions about the ranch. Not until we were riding along the corral fence toward the barn did Grandpa speak again about our mystery. "I'm guessing that you'd rather our womenfolk didn't know about our detective business. Am I right?"

"Don't I need to tell Ma?" I asked.

"Has your conscience been bothering you?" he asked.

"I reckon so," I replied.

"Well, I believe a man who is walking with the Lord should follow his conscience," he said. "I believe a young fellow like you should tell a grown-up family member about something like this. I also believe that your telling me should have satisfied your conscience."

"Thanks, Grandpa," I said. "It did." We agreed to keep quiet about the whole thing until the next day. This would give both of us time to pray and think about things until then...and I would have no more thoughts about dynamite.

Grandma and Grandpa were worn out by the time the supper dishes had been washed, dried and put away. I was glad because Ma didn't have time to notice how tired I was. I quickly excused myself when they did, kissed her good night and got into bed.

I had a lot to think about as I stretched out on the bed. I started praying again; then the next thing I knew I was waking up to the smell of frying bacon. We sat around the table for close to an hour eating biscuits, gravy, bacon and eggs, and drinking coffee. As we laughed and talked, I found myself wishing Pa could have been there.

"I wonder if I might borrow your top hand again today," Grandpa requested as he finished his coffee and pushed his chair away from the table. "I'd like to take a look at this town of yours, and I need a guide."

"Oh, I think we can run this ranch for one more day without him," said Ma. "Could I persuade you two to take the buckboard and pick up some supplies while you're in town? I have a list of things I need, and Grubby should have one ready too. He'll probably be glad to have someone else go to town for a change."

"Why, we'd be happy to help, Lizzie," replied Grandpa. "Arty, I'll get the team hitched while you check with your cook. I believe we're going to have another hot day, so the sooner we leave, the better."

Something like three quarters of an hour later, Grandpa and I headed for White Rock. Grandpa had handed me the reins as soon as I climbed on the seat beside him. "I've been driving for months," he said, "and I'm ready to give someone else a turn."

I didn't mind. Driving the team could get boring

sometimes, but not with Grandpa along. He pulled a harmonica from his pocket and played some songs that he had taught me when I was little. I sang along, and we laughed and talked about the past.

A little more than a mile from town he asked, "Well, did you wake up with any answers this morning?"

"No sir. But I'm rested and should be able to think better."

"So am I," he said. "I believe we were pondering the question of why anyone would pin a Ranger badge on a dead man. What do you think?"

"I reckon someone wanted people to think a Ranger was dead," I answered.

"Or that an outlaw was still alive?"

"Whoa!" I said, pulling back on the reins until the team stopped. "Why? That doesn't make any sense!"

"No, it doesn't, boy; but you can bet it makes sense to this marshal of yours."

"What are we going to do?" I asked.

"Why, we're going to pick up supplies. Then you're going to show me the town, introduce me to your pardner, Jasper, and his family, and then to your marshal."

"That's all?" I questioned.

"Certainly not." Grandpa's spectacles had slid down his nose from the bouncing of the buckboard. Looking over the top of them, he smiled at me. "We're going to keep our eyes and ears open. Of course, we won't learn anything just sitting here."

I clucked to the team and shook the reins once, and they started forward at a trot. This was going to be a very interesting visit to town.

CHAPTER THIRTEEN

We stopped the buckboard in front of the store and went in. Mr. Wilson was waiting on a customer. Grandpa and I walked around, looking at the supplies.

"Hey, Mister," said a familiar voice as Grandpa reached the end of an aisle.

"Are you talking to me?" asked Grandpa.

"Yes sir," said Jasper, stepping into the aisle and pointing at me. "I'm going to have to ask you to leave your hound outside." He spread his feet, hooked his thumbs in his suspenders and squinted at Grandpa. "I won't have a hound in my store, knocking things over, shedding fleas and slobbering all over my mercy dice."

"Do you mean *merchandise?*" asked Grandpa.

Jasper let go of his suspenders and put his hands on his hips. "Are you mocking me, Mister?"

"Why, no," said Grandpa. He looked at me and winked. "I just wanted to make sure that I understood you. Now, as to bringing my hound into the store, I'll send him outside after you fill him up."

The look on Jasper's face made me want to

laugh out loud, but I bit my lip and pretended to sniff some axe handles. I looked at Grandpa's serious expression and knew a whopper was coming.

Jasper's eyes were bulging, and his mouth was hanging open. He looked from me to Grandpa. "Fill him up with what?" he asked.

Grandpa looked surprised. "Why, beans, of course! This can't be the first bean dog you've ever seen. I thought you'd recognize him by that sad, dumb expression on his face."

I looked away again and put my hand over my mouth to keep from laughing out loud. Grandpa kept on. "Any man who travels far from home needs a good bean dog. He does for the man what a canteen does for water. Before you start on a journey, you fill him plumb full of beans. Some trappers I know like to throw in bacon too—just for flavor, you know."

When I turned to look again, Grandpa was sitting on a keg and looking right into Jasper's eyes. Jasper's mouth was still open, his eyes still bulging. "Then after a fellow has been on the trail for a spell, he holds his plate in front of that bean dog with one hand and pumps its tail with the other. That bean dog opens his mouth and fills the plate with hot beans."

Jasper folded his skinny arms across his chest and looked from Grandpa to me. Squinting at Grandpa again, he said, "Mister, I don't reckon a dog can be made full of beans."

Grandpa tapped Jasper's chest with a long, bony finger. "I think you're right, but I've heard that some boy named Jasper Wilson is full of beans!"

When we had finally stopped laughing, I noticed that Mr. Wilson was standing behind Jasper. I don't know how much of Grandpa's story he had heard, but he was still laughing when he shook Grandpa's hand and introduced himself.

We left the list of supplies we needed with Mr. Wilson. He promised that he and Jasper would have everything loaded into the wagon by the time we got back.

I took Grandpa to the bank and introduced him to Mr. Pelham, the bank president. Grandpa said he'd come back in a week or so and open an account.

We left the bank and walked past the general store and the saloon to the hotel. Mr. and Mrs. Mathis were happy to meet Grandpa. They invited us to come back to the hotel dining room for our noon meal. If I hadn't already known that Mrs. Mathis was a good cook, I'd have guessed it, for Mr. and Mrs. Mathis were both rather plump. We promised to return in an hour.

We crossed the street to the building that doubled as both church and school. I was surprised to find the door open. I knocked and heard someone answer. I was really surprised when we found Miss Ross inside. Her hair was pulled back in a bun, and she was sitting at her desk with an open book in front of her. She smiled at me, but I just stood with my mouth open until she spoke. "Hello, Arty. Are you enjoying your summer?"

"Yes ma'am, I am," I replied. "Why are you here? I mean…"

"I'm making plans for the next school year," she said, still smiling. "Have you brought me a new student?"

Blushing, I introduced her to Grandpa. As we walked away, Grandpa grinned at me. "No wonder you like school so much!" he said.

Doc O'Leary had left a note on his door that said he had gone to the Simms ranch to check on a sick child and might not return until the following day.

Mr. Whitman, the barber, was sitting in a chair

outside his shop, reading a book and dozing in the hot sun. He was a skinny little man, not much bigger than me. Beads of sweat were shining on his bald head. I judged he was about Grandpa's age, and they liked each other from the start.

Next, we walked into the funeral parlor. The sign on the door read "T. A. Talbot, Undertaker." Mr. Talbot was average in height, and stocky. He had white hair and a warm smile, and he knew more funny stories than anyone else I have ever met. He made me a little nervous sometimes though. I thought when he looked at me he was measuring me for a coffin.

Bob Taylor, who ran the livery and did some blacksmithing, didn't like having youngsters anywhere near his business, so I told Grandpa about the stable and pointed it out to him.

Our last stop was the marshal's office. I had a knot forming in my stomach as we got closer to his office. For the first time since I had met the marshal, I was nervous about seeing him.

Marshal Bodie was in his office cleaning his rifle. I couldn't help noticing that he seemed nervous about meeting Grandpa. Since the marshal usually ate his lunch at the hotel when he was in town, the three of us walked there together. By the time we sat down at the table, Marshal Bodie was back to normal. Grandpa had a way of putting people at ease.

Miss Ross and Mr. Talbot showed up for their

noon meal too. I knew the grown folks would stay at the table and visit awhile after they had eaten. I ate fast and then asked to be excused. I had work to do.

Walking as fast as I could without drawing attention to myself, I headed for the marshal's office. Grandpa had said the "Wanted" poster might be important, and this might be my only chance to get another look at it. When I got to the marshal's office, I stepped inside and closed the door. For a few seconds I stood with my back against the door, listening. Then I crossed the room to the old desk and opened the drawer where I had seen Marshal Bodie put the stack of "Wanted" posters.

The one I wanted was right on top of the stack. I studied the picture and read the description again. Closing my eyes, I tried to see the dead man's face, this time with a beard. Suddenly I understood why the face had been two colors. He had shaved his beard, and the skin that had been covered by hair was still lighter than the skin that had been tanned by the sun. Had the man shaved his beard, or had someone else shaved it after he was dead? I shuddered and dropped the poster. I bent down, picked it up and read the description one more time.

Just as I reached to put the poster back into the drawer, the office door burst open.

CHAPTER FOURTEEN

The expression "caught red-handed" filled my head. I was standing with my back to the door, still holding that poster. I couldn't drop it into the drawer and close it without the marshal knowing what I was doing, and I couldn't think of one good reason for my being there.

I closed my eyes and took a deep breath. As I started to turn around, he spoke. "Oh, ain't Marshal Bodie going to be het up when he finds an escaped bean dog in his office!"

I grabbed the front of Jasper's shirt, pulled him inside and pushed the door shut. "What are you doing here? You scared me half to death!" I hissed between my teeth.

"I'm sorry, Arty," he whispered. His eyes were bulging so much I thought they might pop out and roll across the floor like marbles. "Me and Pa were finished loading your buckboard. We wasn't busy, so he said I could go around town with you and your grandpa—if you didn't mind. I was coming to look for you when I seen you come in here."

He stopped and squinted at me. "What *are* you doing here? Are you planning to bust someone out of jail? Can I help? We ca—"

"Jasper!" I interrupted, forgetting to whisper. "Is anybody *in* jail?"

"No," he said, looking at the floor.

"Then why would I be bust...I mean, breaking someone *out* of jail?"

Jasper put his hands on his hips and leaned forward, still squinting. "Don't ask me! You're the one that's sneaking around in here, planning to bust someone out."

"I'm *not* planning to bust someone out of jail!" I said. Then I remembered where we were and said, "I'll tell you what I was doing, but first let's get out of here!"

Jasper opened the door and started out. He stopped, backed up and closed it again, bumping into me hard.

"What's wrong with you?" I asked. I felt my bottom lip where the back of Jasper's head had hit it.

"Does the marshal know you're here?" he asked.

"No, why?" I whispered.

"Because he just came out of the hotel, and he's heading this way. Want to hide behind the door and scare him the way we did Tom Green?" asked Jasper.

"No!" I said, grabbing Jasper's arm. "Come on!"

As fast as we could, we crossed the room and opened the back door. I pushed Jasper through first. I started to shut the door but stopped. Just above my head on the inside of the door someone had used a jackknife to fasten a piece of paper. Written on it in pencil was, "Coyote Canyon, midnight."

"Arty, hurry!" Jasper was still speaking very softly.

I closed the door as quietly as I could. We both ran behind the buildings until we came to the alley between Doc O'Leary's office and the school. We slowed to a walk and crossed the street to the hotel.

Grandpa stood up when we walked into the dining room. He thanked Mr. and Mrs. Mathis for the

hearty meal which they wouldn't let him pay for, and we left the hotel.

When we got into the buckboard, Grandpa checked to make sure everything was packed well enough to make the trip home. When he had finished, he turned to Jasper. "Well done, Mr. Wilson. Please have your father add these things to Mrs. Anderson's account. Here's a little something for you." Grandpa pulled a nickel from his pocket and tossed it to Jasper. He missed catching it but picked it up and wiped it on his pants. With eyes bulging, he thanked Grandpa and turned to run into the store.

"Jasper!" said Grandpa. Jasper stopped and turned to face Grandpa. "Don't waste any of that money on a bean dog. I haven't found one yet that was worth a nickel."

Jasper grinned and waved. As I clucked to the team and we started out of town, he turned and ran back into the store.

Grandpa chuckled. "I reckon Jasper provides plenty of entertainment. Of course, you probably do a good job yourself, don't you?"

"I have no idea what you are talking about," I answered.

"I see," said Grandpa. I knew without looking at him that he was grinning. "Mind if I ask what you two were up to while I was finishing my lunch and enjoying the company of my new friends?"

I swallowed hard and kept looking straight

ahead. "What makes you think we were up to something?" I asked, trying unsuccessfully to sound innocent.

Grandpa looked at me, then said, "Remember that your grandmother and I reared your three uncles and one aunt, as well as your mother, so we are veterans, my boy, and very hard to fool. Boys who have just done something secretive have a certain look about them, and you and Jasper had that look when you came to the hotel. Is there something you need to tell me?"

I had reckoned that with Ma, Marshal Bodie, Miss Ross, Chad, Grubby and the other two hands, Bill and Bo, watching, I didn't have much of a chance to get away with anything because I was outnumbered. Now I was learning that Grandpa outnumbered me all by himself.

I let the team go at their own pace. Then I told Grandpa how I'd figured out why the dead man's face was two colors, then about the note on the door.

He sat with his eyes closed and said nothing. I supposed he must have gone to sleep, but after about fifteen minutes, he opened his eyes and looked directly at me. "What are we going to do? You're sure this marshal of yours is square?"

"I'm sure," I said, "and so is Ma. She's sure enough that she..." I stopped.

"That she *what?*" asked Grandpa.

"That she...she really trusts him." I hoped that my tan was dark enough to hide the red in my face from Grandpa. He said nothing. "He's square," I continued, trying to change the subject. If Ma wanted Grandpa and Grandma to know how much she and Marshal Bodie liked each other, she could tell them herself.

"Then why is he invited to Coyote Canyon at midnight?" asked Grandpa. "You did leave the note there, didn't you? The fact that it was there means he hadn't seen it yet."

"I left the note," I said. "It almost has to be from the outlaw—or whoever the man is. How can we know why he's going or who he's meeting?"

"*Whom* he's meeting," Grandpa said. "We can't know unless we're there. If you and your ma had doubts about the marshal, I'd say he might be crooked and needs to be stopped. As it stands, he more likely needs help. He doesn't sound like a fool, but the best of men are sometimes too proud to ask for help."

"Or maybe they're not always sure who can be trusted," I added.

We were coming through the wide gate to the ranch, and Grandpa said, "Arty, you may be onto something. When we get to the house, let me do the talking."

The more I thought about that plan, the more I liked it. In fact, I reckon I was overjoyed.

CHAPTER FIFTEEN

Grandpa climbed down from the buckboard and went into the house. I drove the team to the front of the cookhouse and stopped. Something like an hour later I had finished helping Grubby unload the supplies. Then I put the buckboard away, unhitched the team and fed them some oats.

When I walked into the parlor, all three grown-ups stopped talking and looked at me. I wanted to turn around and light a shuck for Mexico. Ma and Grandma both looked scared and worried. It was Grandpa's grin that gave me the courage to walk on in. I sat on the hearth near his chair and waited.

"I told the women everything," said Grandpa. He must have seen the anger in my eyes, for he held up one hand, the palm toward me. "Now, before you lose your temper, hear me out. I've known these two ladies for a long time, Son. I respect their opinions, and I love them too much to go behind their backs any longer. Your ma agrees with you that the marshal is a straight shooter. She also agrees with me that pride sometimes clouds the judgment of even the best men."

Grandpa took out his bandanna, then took off his spectacles and wiped his face. I waited, knowing he wasn't finished. I quietly watched as he put on his spectacles, folded the bandanna and put it back in his pocket. Then looking straight at me, he continued: "These women agreed that the marshal might need someone to back his play tonight. They also think that I'm a little old to be that someone and you're a little too young." He held up his hand again when I started to argue. "Hold your horses; I'm not finished. I believe that I've managed to persuade them that although they may be right about us separately, together we add up to one pretty good man. Besides, with your ranch hands taking that herd to Dodge City, we're the only men available for the job. Your ma tells me that before Bill left, he said he reckoned nothing would come up that you couldn't handle."

"You mean we're going to Coyote Canyon tonight?" I asked, jumping up from the hearth.

Ma and Grandma still looked worried.

"As soon as we can get our gear together!" Grandpa said; then he added, "Oh, I'm forgetting one thing."

"What?" I asked, feeling the beginning of another knot in my stomach.

"Son, I haven't asked you if you want to go."

I let out the breath I had been holding. "I reckon we're pards," I said. I couldn't keep back that grin!

We were ready to go in an hour, although it only took me fifteen minutes to saddle Prince and Sally. Grandpa had used that time to gather the things he thought we might need. We spent the next forty-five minutes listening to our womenfolk warning us to be careful. Grandpa and I had to promise to stay hidden and not take any chances. Grandpa said we would, unless circumstances got out of control. I suspect neither Ma nor Grandma cared much for that assurance, but they were stuck with it.

As we left the ranch and headed for Coyote Canyon, my heart was pounding, and my throat was drier than usual. Again I could feel a knot beginning to form in my stomach.

"Where's the best place for us to be?" asked Grandpa.

"For what?" I asked.

"Well, there's going to be a full moon tonight. We need a place where we'll be hidden but able to see as much as possible. Chances are good that we'll watch whatever happens, then go home. If we do need to help the marshal, I need to be where I can do him some good." Grandpa leaned forward and patted the butt of the old Sharps buffalo gun which he carried across his saddle.

Suddenly my throat was so dry that I couldn't swallow. "Grandpa, how will we know where the marshal will be?"

"We won't, boy," he replied in almost a whisper.

"That's why you need to guess the most likely place to meet someone. You know the canyon far better than I do."

I tried to swallow, but my throat was so dry it felt like it was full of sand. "What if I'm wrong?" I asked.

"Try to pick a place that will let us move around

a little," Grandpa answered quietly. "Take your time, Son. We have a good four hours until sundown. I reckon whoever the marshal's meeting won't come until right around then. He'll not want to be seen riding in, but he might need to see where he's going. If he's not in the canyon by sundown, I judge he'll hole up until the moon rises. It should be up before the marshal rides in. Anyway, we need to hide where we can see the mouth of the canyon. The more we can see of the rest of it, the better."

By the time we rode into Coyote Canyon, I'd picked the hiding place. We picketed Prince and Sally out of sight behind some boulders, and I led Grandpa back about twenty yards toward the mouth of the canyon. We climbed fifty feet up a sharp slope to a *mesilla,* a flat spot with boulders scattered around.

"We call this the Tower," I said.

"*We?*" asked Grandpa, raising his eyebrows.

"Me, Jasper, Tom Green—you haven't met him yet—and Esther Travis."

"I don't recall having met Esther either," said Grandpa, winking at me and smiling.

I could feel my cheeks burning as I blushed. "She's just a friend, Grandpa."

"I didn't think she was your wife," he said with a chuckle. He had brought his saddlebags with him. He opened one, took out a telescope and began to look slowly around the canyon. Then without looking at me, he finished his sentence: "...yet."

"Grandpa, she's just a friend!"

"I understand, Arty." He was still studying the canyon through the telescope. "I know just what you mean. When I was your age, I had a friend a lot like Esther."

I felt better to hear him say so. "What was her name?" I asked.

"Oh, let me see now—it was so long ago." He was quiet, still using the telescope. After a minute or so, he said, "I remember what it was—Martha! Martha Strunk. Oh, she was a pretty little thing. Last I heard, she married a good man, had a family and did quite well for herself."

The name *Strunk* opened one of those little doors in the back of my mind. "You're talking about Grandma, aren't you?"

He put the telescope down and answered, "Sure am!"

We climbed down to the horses. They were in the shade, but the canyon was still mighty hot. We had brought two extra canteens—both were twice the size of the one I usually carried. Pouring water from one of them into our hats, we gave Prince and Sally a drink. We got the rest of our gear— food, canteens and bedrolls—but we left our saddles on the horses. Both of us knew we might need to ride in a hurry.

Then we got as comfortable as a person can get when sitting on a rock, and I did one of the hardest things a young cowboy ever has to do—waited.

CHAPTER SIXTEEN

We prayed together, then talked for a while about—well, about the kinds of things any boy and his grandpa would talk about on a warm, sunny afternoon. I told Grandpa about the cattle drive's being later than usual this year because of the flash flood that had come in the middle of the roundup. When it hit, the part of the herd that had already been gathered had scattered, and the roundup had started over. Bill had taken all of the hands and left Grubby behind. Chad and Bo had tried to come up with a reason he'd understand, but Grubby knew why they were taking a younger cook: they were behind schedule and were going to have to push hard to get the herd to Dodge.

"Old Grub would keep up fine," Chad had told me the night before they left. "Bill's just afraid that he'll kill himself doing it. We'll take him next time—and probably you, too!"

I had to work for two days before I could get Grubby to talk to me. He was hot!

Grandpa told some more about the things that had happened on their trip out to see us. I wanted to ask him how long he and Grandma could stay, but I didn't want to think about their leaving.

After a while I guess we both got sleepy. We sat facing each other, our backs against boulders and our hat brims pulled down over our eyes. I made up my mind to rest but to stay awake. The next thing I knew, Grandpa's hand was on my shoulder, shaking me gently.

"I'm sorry, Grandpa."

"Ain't anything to be sorry for, boy. I slept too. Seemed like the best use of our time."

The sun was going to set soon. We fed the horses some oats that we had brought and gave them more water. When we were back in our hiding place, we ate some of the food we had brought along, drank from our canteens...and waited.

Somewhere deeper in the canyon a coyote howled. Farther away, another answered.

The sun had almost set when they came. We heard their horses before we saw them. There were four dusty riders. They rode into the shadows of the canyon, dismounted, then led their tired horses to a place where we could not only see them but hear most of what the riders said.

"I reckon you picked the right spot for us!" Grandpa whispered. Pleased as I was by the compliment, I still had a knot in my stomach.

The next few hours passed quickly, probably because I had such an uncommon interest in what I was watching.

The men unsaddled their horses and built a

fire; one of them made coffee. When I looked at Grandpa, he rubbed his stomach, then made a sad face and pointed to his canteen. There would be no coffee for us tonight.

After the sun set, one of them fried some bacon and then stirred in a bunch of beans. The men sat around the fire. For a while all we could hear was the sound of knives and spoons scraping tin plates. Now and then someone let out a big belch.

When they had finished eating, one man took out a pipe and began to tamp tobacco into its bowl. Two others were rolling cigarettes. The fourth one took off his hat and stretched out on his back, resting his head on his saddle and folding his hands across his stomach.

The shadows and hat brims had kept me from getting a good look at their faces until now. I had seen this man's face somewhere before. Suddenly a chill ran down my spine, and the hair on the back of my neck stood up. I borrowed Grandpa's telescope. When I focused it on the man's face, I was sure it was the face from the "Wanted" poster: Scott Cooley!

I backed away from the edge of the *mesilla,* and Grandpa followed. I told him who the outlaw was. "Why would Marshal Bodie meet Scott Cooley like this?" I wondered aloud.

"If we knew that," he whispered, "we wouldn't be hiding up here. I have a feeling we're about to find out."

For the next three hours the camp was quiet. Three of the outlaws slept while a Mexican I had heard Cooley call Rodriguez kept the fire going and stood watch. As the moon rose, Rodriguez let the fire burn down a little. He wandered around for a while, then he sat on one of the smaller boulders, rolled another cigarette and lit it. The brim of his sombrero hid the glow of the tip, but the smell of burning tobacco was strong.

Suddenly Rodriguez threw his cigarette on the ground and stepped on it. *"Amigos,"* he said softly.

I looked from him to the fire, but the bedrolls were empty. I looked back to where Rodriguez had been; he also had vanished. What happened next went a lot faster than I can tell it.

A rider came into sight in the moonlight. He was hurt or sick or something because he sagged in the saddle. He was hunched forward over the saddle horn, but he straightened a little as he neared the fire. I recognized him as the outlaw that Jasper and I had seen here before—the one Marshal Bodie had met in his office.

"Cooley! Rodriguez! Sandy!" he called in a raspy voice. "Come out, come out, wherever you are! I got some good sippin' whiskey!"

I looked at Grandpa, who mouthed the word "drunk." As we watched, the man took a long drink from a large brown jug he had been holding in front of him on the saddle. When he finished his drink, he tried to put the bottle back on the saddle but missed. The weight of the jug pulled him off balance, and he fell, landing on his stomach. He tried to get up but sank down again. He lay still with his face resting on one arm.

Rodriguez came out first. He spun his revolver on one finger and slipped it back into its holster. Walking over to the man, he stooped and picked up the jug. By some miracle it had not broken. He took a long drink and then, facing the fire, held up the jug. "Hey, amigos! Billy has forgotten that gringos cannot hold their whiskey. I could finish this jug myself, but I will share it with you because you are my compadres." After taking another drink, he walked toward the fire.

Two of the other outlaws hurried out of the shadows, and each took a long drink. The newcomer still hadn't moved. The three men started toward the fire when Rodriguez stopped. "Hey, Carter," he said, tugging the sleeve of one of the men, "help me drag Billy closer to the fire. We don't want him to get cold tonight."

"You're right," said Carter, "especially since he brought us some whiskey to keep *us* warm."

Grandpa and I could see everything that was happening in the bright moonlight. When Rodriguez started to roll Billy over, Billy sprang to his feet. He was definitely not drunk, and the six-gun in his hand covered Rodriguez and Carter. "You ain't Billy!" Carter roared.

The third outlaw, who was already back at the

fire, dropped the jug, turned and crouched, holding his gun.

"Drop it or die!" ordered a familiar voice.

I didn't know about Grandpa, but I reckon my heart stopped long enough to miss a beat or two.

Marshal Bodie stood between two boulders on the other side of the fire, his rifle leveled at the outlaw. Only when the outlaw dropped his gun did the marshal step into the open. The pretend drunk had disarmed the other two and was herding them toward the fire.

I had started to relax when Grandpa squeezed my arm so hard I almost screamed in pain. "Where's Cooley?" he whispered in my ear. Seconds later, the "drunk" stranger asked the same question.

Carter smiled one of those buzzard-like smiles and asked, "Who's Cooley?"

I wanted to yell out a warning, but Grandpa held a finger to his lips. "We have the edge," he said. "Cooley doesn't know we're here. Keep your eyes open. When he makes a play, we have to be ready. Since he doesn't know about us, he's likely to make a mistake."

Not more than a minute or two later, Cooley made his move.

CHAPTER SEVENTEEN

I'm not bragging; I'm just telling you what happened. Cooley was circling around behind the marshal, and no one in the group at the fire could see him. Grandpa and I could because we were above him.

"What are you going to do?" I whispered.

"I'll see if I can bark him," Grandpa replied.

Now, I'd seen Pa bark squirrels before. He'd take a rifle and knock a squirrel out of a tree without shooting it through the body and ruining a good part of the meat. The point was to stun the squirrel by grazing him with the bullet. I knew Grandpa had a bigger target than a squirrel, but he was farther away, had only moonlight to see by and was using a .52 caliber buffalo gun.

"I'll only get one shot," he said, "so I'd better make it a good one."

He quickly pulled off his bandanna and spectacles and dried his face. As he brought his hand up to replace his spectacles, they caught on a button on the front of his shirt and slipped out of his hands. The moon was plenty bright around us, but the place where we were hiding was in the shadow of a half dozen large boulders.

The look on Grandpa's face made me sick. "Arty, I can't even see him without my spectacles!"

"What are we going to do?" I asked.

"Don't move," ordered Grandpa. "You might step on my spectacles. I didn't hear any glass breaking, so they may be undamaged. We have to find them now, though, or—"

"Or what?" I broke in.

"Or you'll have to take the shot."

"Grandpa, I can't shoot a strange gun well enough to bark Cooley."

"You won't be trying to bark him," he said. "Where is he now?"

I checked. Cooley was still moving quietly, like a cougar stalking its prey. "He's still on the move," I replied.

"We may only have seconds," said Grandpa. "Pray, Arty, and find those spectacles."

I prayed silently and tried to keep my hands from shaking as I felt around for the spectacles.

"It's no good, Arty; we're out of time," said Grandpa. "You know how to shoot a rifle. This one is going to kick a lot more, so hang on."

Shaking badly, I took off my bandanna and wiped sweat and tears from my face. I didn't want to shoot anybody, but Marshal Bodie would die if I didn't.

I found Cooley in the rocks again. He was

straight across the fire from us, looking for a place that would give him a clear shot and still protect him from returned fire. I took a deep breath and looked through the rear sight.

"I found them!" Grandpa said in a low voice. "They're not broken. Give me the gun."

I wiped my eyes with my sleeve. Grandpa shot and Cooley spun around. His rifle flew into the air and then clattered on the rocks below him.

The marshal and the stranger looked first at the rifle, then at the spot where we were. "Nice shot, Mr. Delaney!" said Marshal Bodie. "You and Arty can come out now. I think the show is over, and I'm ready for some sleep."

I looked at Grandpa. He raised his eyebrows

and shrugged his shoulders. "Don't ask me how he knew. I sure didn't tell him!"

By the time we had gathered our gear, loaded it back on Prince and Sally and ridden around to the fire, the marshal and the stranger had all four outlaws in handcuffs. The stranger had just finished tying Cooley's bandanna around a wound in the outlaw's arm. Grandpa's wink told me that he'd barked Cooley just the way he'd wanted to.

"Arty, Mr. Delaney, say hello to Texas Ranger George Arrington," said Marshal Bodie.

"It's a pleasure," he said, shaking Grandpa's hand, then mine. "We're much obliged to you two for saving our bacon tonight."

"Arty," said the marshal, "I know you're so full of questions that you're about to pop. Ranger Arrington and I will take these *hombres* back to town and lock them up; then we'll all get a good night's sleep. Tomorrow we'll ride out to the ranch and answer all of your questions."

We rode out of Coyote Canyon together, then said good night. Grandpa and I headed for the ranch, and the two lawmen herded their prisoners toward town.

"I don't know about you, boy," sighed Grandpa, "but I've had about all the day I can stand!"

Right then I reckon we were more tired than we were excited. I don't know when I dozed off, but when I woke up, Prince and I were stopped at the corral. Grandpa was a few feet behind me, slumped forward and snoring, still in the saddle. I slid off Prince's back and walked to Sally. I tapped Grandpa's leg, and he opened his eyes. "Would you like to trade this horse for a feather bed?" I asked.

"I'd trade her for a blanket on the ground at the moment," he replied, grinning. He groaned a little as he stepped down from the saddle and began to stretch. "No offense intended, Sally," he said, patting her neck. "You, sir," he said, handing me the reins, "have a deal."

I'm sure that Sally and Prince went to sleep a long time before Grandpa and I did. They didn't have two women waiting to hear what had happened.

CHAPTER EIGHTEEN

When the marshal and Ranger Arrington rode out to the ranch the next afternoon, I hadn't been awake for much more than an hour. Ma and Grandma had coffee and dried-apple pie ready. The six of us were sitting at the table when the Ranger started his story.

"I'd been trailing Scott Cooley and his sidekicks for quite a spell. They were headed south. Cooley always avoided taking his gang into town unless they were there to do a job. He'd have them ride around the town and then send a man back for supplies. He figured that way hardly anybody knew where he was."

"Did his plan work?" asked Grandpa.

"Well enough that he escaped capture for over three years," the Ranger replied, "and not just from us. He had other lawmen, bounty hunters and even Pinkerton men after him. It's hard to catch a man when you don't know where he is."

Grandma served the Ranger a second piece of pie and refilled his coffee cup. He took a bite of the pie and chewed with his eyes closed. After taking a long drink of the hot coffee, he looked at

Grandma and said with a smile, "If you ever decide to join the Rangers, Ma'am, make sure you get into Company A.

"Now where was I? Oh, I remember. Cooley's gang had been avoiding going into towns as a group. They skirted a little place north of here called Benton. I stopped in town to telegraph headquarters so they'd know which way I was headed. After sending the telegram, I stopped by the dry goods store to get some coffee and a box of cartridges. When I came out of the store, Billy Nelson, the only man in Cooley's outfit who knew me by sight, was riding up the middle of the street. He was looking right at me, so I couldn't hide. He turned his horse around and lit a shuck to get back to the gang."

"Why didn't you shoot him?" I asked.

"I drew my gun," he said, shaking his head, "but there were too many townsfolk who might have gotten hurt...or killed."

After another bite of pie and a swallow of coffee, he got back to his story. "I dumped my supplies into a saddlebag and went after him. I had no way of knowing when or where Billy was supposed to meet the others. I did know that if I lost the element of surprise, I'd lose my chance to catch Cooley.

"I lost his trail at sunset and made camp for the night. I didn't know the country well enough to keep riding, and I reckoned Billy didn't either."

The Ranger ate the last of his pie, finished his

coffee, wiped his mouth with his bandanna, then looked across the table at me.

"I found his trail at first light and saw his dust just after sunrise. I was half a mile behind him when his horse fell and got a large cut on its side. Billy rode it on up into that canyon where you and your little pardner found me, Arty."

"Coyote Canyon," I said.

"That's the place," he replied. "When he got into the rocks and saw how badly the horse was hurt, he shot it in the head and hid from me there. I tried to talk Billy into giving himself up, but he kept answering me with bullets. After I shot him, I worked my way through the rocks and found him the way you saw him. He was dead, and I had no idea of where to find Cooley and the others."

"And that's when Jasper and I showed up?" I asked.

"No, son, you two showed up a couple of hours later," said the Ranger. "I was sitting there on a boulder, trying to decide what to do, when I smelled smoke. Working my way back into the canyon, I found a deserted camp. The fire was still smoking, and there was a note with a rock to hold it down. This is it."

The Ranger handed me a wrinkled, stained scrap of paper. Someone had written in large letters with a pencil:

Got a job to do—wait here. Thursday midnight. S. C.

I read the note out loud.

When I was finished, Ranger Arrington took up the story again. "Once I knew that Cooley and the rest of the gang were camping in the canyon, I knew why Billy hadn't given up. He figured his pardners would hear the shooting and come to his rescue. He didn't know they had left. Now that I knew when and where to find the rest of the gang, I had a couple of things that needed doing."

"What were they?" I asked.

"I had to get to White Rock and ask Luke for help. We'd worked together a time or two, and I knew I could count on him. I also needed to keep anyone from finding out that I was around or that Billy had been killed. I figured I'd need Luke's help there too. I couldn't chance having someone recognize Billy, and I couldn't be sure that Cooley and his boys weren't in White Rock. I shaved off his beard with my Bowie knife. Then I traded hats with him and meant to trade six-guns—he carried a fancy one that someone might have recognized. That's when I noticed his holster was empty. He only had his Winchester."

"That's the gun Jasper found!" I said.

"Yep," answered the Ranger, "and I was some kind of glad to get it! Anyway, without his beard, I didn't think his own mother would recognize him. If the gang didn't know he was dead, I thought I could make Cooley think I was Billy long enough to get the drop on him. Just to muddy the waters a little more, I pinned my badge on him—"

"Right through the skin!" I hastened to add. Ma put her hand over her mouth and gasped.

"I didn't mean to do that," said the Ranger, "but I reckon he was past feeling anything. I was looking around for that six-gun when you two boys arrived. I didn't mean to scare you, but I needed you to think you'd found a live outlaw and a dead Ranger."

"We did," I said, "at first. Where did you go when you left?"

"I hid in the rocks near the mouth of the canyon and waited for you two to leave. I figured you boys would go tell the marshal about the dead body and he'd be riding out pretty quick, so I found a place where I could see who was coming into the canyon. Then I waited."

"That's where I came in," said Marshal Bodie. "I went out there to look at a dead body, but I found a live one sitting on a boulder and waiting for me. George told me what he needed, and I got busy. I went back to town, got a buckboard and made sure plenty of folks saw me bringing in the body of the 'Ranger.'"

"Then I rode into town late that night," said the Ranger, "so that I could get my own gear back without being seen. I still would wear Billy's hat and gun to get as close to Cooley's fire as possible, and Luke would watch my back from the rocks. We figured the two of us could take them."

"Then yesterday morning I couldn't remember if I'd told Luke the right day," continued the Ranger. "I slipped into town and came through the back door. No one was there, so I left a note—the one you and Jasper found."

"Fortunately," said Marshal Bodie, "you left the note where you found it. I showed up, and you know the rest."

"Not *all* the rest, Marshal. How'd you know we were in the rocks?"

"I got there a split second before you and your grandpa, and I saw you ride in. I figured what you were up to, so I thought it best just to let it play out."

"We were lucky that Arty and Mr. Delaney were there," said the Ranger.

"It wasn't luck, George," stated Marshal Bodie. "It was God's working from start to finish!"

"Uh, speaking of finish," said the Ranger, pushing his chair back, "I'm finished here. I need to hit the saddle and start back toward headquarters. Thank you for the coffee and the pie. It was a pleasure to make your acquaintance, ladies."

He shook hands with Grandpa and with me and then with the marshal, and we all walked outside. The marshal and the Ranger both swung into their saddles.

"I have to get back to town," said the marshal. "I'll see you in a day or two."

That night we sat in the parlor, talking about how God had kept us safe. Just as Grandpa had finished praying that God would protect the hands, they came home from the cattle drive.

No one said anything for a minute or two, and then Grandma spoke.

"Lizzy, your father and I have something we'd like to discuss with you. It concerns the matter of our return to Kentucky."

"Mother, you can't be thinking of leaving for at least two months. I wish you'd—"

"Hear me out," interrupted Grandma.

Ma was getting those red blotches on her neck that meant she was either scared or mad or maybe both. I felt a knot in my stomach.

"We didn't say anything in our letter because we wanted to talk to you and Artemus in person."

I was really beginning to get worried. Grandma had red spots on her neck too.

"This is a bit awkward," she said quietly, "but we sold our farm before we came out here."

"You did *what?*" Ma asked.

"We thought we might become Texans," said Grandpa, "if we could find someone to put us up."

Ma was smiling again with tears running down her cheeks. I was jumping up and down and whooping like a wild man! And after all that had happened since we'd gotten that letter from them, there I was again wondering if I'd ever understand women. I reckoned that was just one more area where I was going to need God's help.

For a complete list of books available from the Sword of the Lord, write to Sword of the Lord Publishers, P. O. Box 1099, Murfreesboro, Tennessee 37133.

(800) 251–4100
(615) 893–6700
FAX (615) 848–6943
www.swordofthelord.com